Dr. Image

J. M. Willis

Copyright @ J.M. Willis Books

Cover photo shutterstock/CURAphotography.com

This is a work of fiction, names, characters, places, businesses, events, and incidents are either a product of the author's imagination or used in a fictitious manner. Any resemblance to actual persons, living or dead or actual events is purely coincidental.

Some situations or language are not suitable for children under the age of eighteen.

Dr. Image

My new client is big trouble, in a bad way. As his publicist, it's my job to keep him out of the spotlight. At least anything that would ruin his already bad image. How can I do that and keep my job? He has me all hot and bothered and I have no idea what to do. Dr. Sexy is bad for both of our reputations.

Chapter One

The universe has just taken a huge crap all over me. My power went out because I don't have the money to pay for it and they won't give me anymore extensions. So, I overslept and now I'm going to be late for work. I'm so glad I took a shower last night and can save time by skipping a freezing cold one this morning. I run around my two bedroom apartment like a crazy person using the light on my cell phone to find my clothes and car keys.

After about ten minutes, I'm flying out the door. I rush to get into my car. Relief hits me when it starts; I might just make it to work on time. But my happy mood plummets when it starts shaking and not going more than five miles an hour. I've only made it one block from my apartment. I pull over and get out. "This can't be happening to me!" I yell, when I see I have a flat tire.

I pull up the Uber app on my phone. Then request a car to pick me up. Luckily, I can see the address on the house I pulled over in front of. I quickly type it in and see there is an Uber ten minutes away from me. So, I push the request car button and wait for it to come. While I wait, I text my secretary and friend Sarah, to hold down the fort until I get there. Just as I push send, my cell phone dies. "Fuck!"

I'm starting to panic, what if that cancels my Uber request? What if Sarah didn't get my text? I can't even look up the Uber rules to see what happens if your phone dies. How am I going to pay for it? Maybe I should turn around and head home, I can still see my apartment complex from here. I can call Sarah and tell her I'll be late. Crap, I can't even do that with no power on. I open my car door and grab my phone charger.

A few minutes later a car pulls up in front of me and rolls down the window. "Did you call for an Uber?" A man asks. "Yes, I need to get to work. Can you take me to Image, in downtown LA?" I ask him hoping he will drive that far. "I guess if I have to." Then he rolls his eyes at me as he slowly gets out and opens my door. This man must be over three hundred pounds and his shirt has ketchup stains on it. But with no other options, I get in his back seat.

The car makes a creaking noise when he gets in and the whole car smells like cigarette smoke. I try to hold my breath. "Can I plug in my charger? My phone just died." He smiles in the rearview mirror and you can see food in his teeth. Oh my god, this guy needs a bath and a toothbrush. "That will be an extra five dollar charge." That is ridiculous, it doesn't cost him anything for me to charge my phone. Without any other options, I pass the USB cord up for him to plug it in. Then I give him the address for work.

We are finally on our way. Even if we don't hit too much

traffic, I'm still going to be thirty minutes late. I can't afford to lose this job. Mr. Harrison, the founder and CEO of the hottest public relations company in Los Angeles is such a hard ass. He built the company from the ground up. We have helped some of the top A-list names in Hollywood become famous. I had just graduated from UCLA with a bachelor's degree in public relations when Mr. Harrison hired me four years ago, straight out of college. I've been working on my master's degree and working full time ever since I graduated. Hence, why I don't have any money to pay my power bill or a tow truck.

Suddenly I'm engulfed in the worst smell and I start gagging. Oh my god, he just farted and let me tell you this. It was silent and deadly. I cover my nose, coughing and reach over to open the window. When I push down, nothing happens. "Could you unlock the windows? I need some air." I say through my hand. "Sorry they don't work." You have got to be shiting me, pun intended. This is the worst Uber ride ever, at least that is what I thought. Then he lights a cigarette.

"Really? Can you at least put that out, until I get out of the car?" I ask as I cough more from the smoke filling my lungs. How can people smoke? I can't even breathe. "My car, my rules. I can let you out here and you can get another Uber." He tells me. "We are on the freeway! You can't let me out here." Not that I could even get another Uber, my phone only says five percent. "Just hurry if you can, I'm already late." I pull the jacket of my suit over my face. "Why don't you just shut up and let me drive?" He complains, the nerve of him, this is his job. I suffer the longest ten more minutes of my life.

Finally, he pulls up in front of Image. Our company occupies the top ten stories of a thirty floor high-rise. I get out and turn on my seven percent charged phone to pay for the Uber. "That will be forty-two dollars with the extra five dollars to charge your phone." He states. Then he taps his dirty fingers on a sign on his dashboard, 'tips are appreciated.' He can't be serious. I punch in the forty-two dollar amount and pay him. "Here's your tip, take a bath!" He flips me off and I yell. "Asshole! Then I hurry into the building.

Chapter Two

I make it to the elevator when the door is closing. "Hold the door!" I yell just as it shuts. I frantically tap the button to call another one. Five more minutes pass as I wait. Finally, it dings, and I step in. I pull out my compact and check my hair and makeup. "You might as well pack up your things and leave. Save yourself the humiliation of being fired." I would recognize the stupid little twats voice anywhere. "Becky what's the matter? Did John turn you down again?" I say sarcastically back. This is the only way to deal with Becky. The office slut that has slept her way to the top and is trying to get my promotion. I'm sick of her always perfectly pressed clothes and size two body. It is enough to make anyone envious. But there is no way I'm letting her take my job, not when I'm way better at it than she is.

"Nope, he is taking me out tonight. The promotion is as good as mine." My eyes widen. If he gives her a promotion, I'm quitting. No way am I going to work with her as my boss. "I'm sure he will fire you when he gets gonorrhea from you." That shuts her up and the elevator door finally opens. I leave a stunned Becky behind. Maybe she really does have it. I was just pulling her leg.

My office is on the twenty-ninth floor. Only executives and partners are on the top floor. While I may not be up there yet; I do have my own office. Sarah's desk sits just outside my door. She is waiting there now. "I know, I know I'm late. I've had the worst day of my life. Any messages for me?" Sarah looks me up and down. "Mr. Harrison has been waiting for you in his office." She tells me and I look down at my watch. I am forty minutes late and my boss is waiting, just great.

I rush into my office and put my purse down. Sarah follows me inside. "I told him you were on an important phone call. You should be okay. But you need to change your shoes." I look down. "What the fuck?" I'm wearing one black and one navy pump. I kick them off and reach under my desk for my black flats. It's not something I usually wear around the office. My private office on a long day when my feet hurt yes; outside of it no. I slip them on. "Okay, how do I look?" I ask Sarah and she passes me some lipstick.

"You better hurry." Sarah says and gives me the client folder I've been working on. Then I'm hurrying out the door. As I make my way to Mr. Harrison's office, I leaf through the pages. I'm trying to remember the latest numbers from the billboard charts. Mia is the next biggest pop star. I've been working tirelessly to improve her image. I'm proud of what we have accomplished working together.

Mrs. Grace Peterson, my boss's executive secretary looks up when she sees me. She is older but always wears expensive perfectly tailored clothes. "Anna, I see you finally made it into work today. Are you okay?" She asks concerned. "Crap, does he know I was late? I had a horrible morning." She smiles and whispers.

"Don't worry, I won't tell him. Go on in, he is waiting." I take a deep breath and open the door.

I walk in and the place looks like a museum. Everything shines to perfection and everything is in its rightful spot. Even down to the three pens that sit neatly on his desk. John Harrison II, the CEO of Image, is an older man in his late sixties. He sits proudly behind his mahogany desk in an Armani suit. I'm sure it was tailor made by Armani himself. This guy has more money than he knows what to do with. "You're late Ms. Johnson." I'm not going to lie to him, he could fire me.

"Sorry sir, unexpected problems this morning." I state. "You're paid to expect the unexpected. In this business you have to be one step ahead of everything. I'm not sure you are mature enough to make it in this company anymore." He chastises me. "I'm sorry sir, it won't happen again." He gets up from his desk and starts pacing. Then he stands by me and stares above his desk. I follow his gaze. There is a plaque on the wall behind his desk. The motto of his business 'Image Is Everything", it reads. I look down to my black flats. It's then I smell my clothes, that smell like cigarette smoke from the Uber ride.

"Image is everything. If you can't follow that, I'm going to have to let you go. I can't have my employees showing up looking and smelling like you do." He says sternly. "Mr. Harrison please give me one more chance. It won't happen again, I promise." I plead with him. He stares at me for a moment.

"How do you expect our clients to pay us to improve their image, if you show up looking like this? They would laugh in our face and go to the next company. "Sir, this won't happen again. Did you see the stats on Mia?" I pull out a paper from the folder and show him. "The billboards say she is up to number ten, up from sixty-seven. I'm good at my job Sir. I won't let you down again, you can count on me." He stares at me for a moment.

"Alright Ms. Johnson, I will give you one more chance. But mess this up and I will have no other choice but to fire you." I smile in relief. "Thank you, Sir." I stick my hand out to shake his. He looks down at it, in disgust. I slowly pull it back. "I'm giving you the day off, without pay. Go home and change. And for god's sake, take a shower. I can't have you smelling like this around here." I turn to leave, before he sees the tears in my eyes.

"Oh Ms. Johnson, wait a minute." I turn around and he hands me a folder. "This is the reason I wanted to see you this morning. I have a new client for you. A plastic surgeon that is being sued for malpractice. All the information is in the folder. He is paying us two hundred and fifty thousand to help him. Don't screw this up. It may make you or break you here at Image." Then he turns around dismissing me.

I hurry out of his office and stop at Mrs. Peterson's desk. "Well, how did it go?" She asks in a whisper. "I'm not fired yet, but he is sending me home without pay." She looks sympathetic. "I guess it's good that it's only one day then. I'll see you tomorrow." I wave bye and return to my office. Sarah hands me a cup of coffee on my way in.

"Sarah, shut the door." I place the folder and coffee down, then plop down at my desk in a huff. Sarah does as I ask and joins me, waiting to hear what happened. "I've been working my ass off for this guy for the last four years. Now he is sending me home without pay for a whole day! My power just got turned off and I had the worst Uber driver in history. What am I going to do?" I complain to her.

"So, you're not fired?" She asks me. "No, not yet. I have a new client. He is some plastic surgeon being sued. If I don't improve his image, Mr. Harrison basically said he would let me go." I push the folder her way and, in the process, my coffee cup tips over and I spill my coffee all over it. "Crap!" We both rush to pick up the folder. The coffee is already soaking in. I pull out all of the pages. Then lay them out one by one, on my now dry desk that Sarah has wiped off.

Thankfully only one page is ruined and it's his profile picture. It is a blurry mess. I still have everything else. "Sarah I'm going home before anything else bad happens to me. I wish this day never started." I say in disbelief. How can everything go so wrong? "I thought you said your power was turned off." Sarah reminds me. "I'll just have to live with no power and cold showers until Friday when we get paid." Her eyebrows shoot up in surprise.

"You can't live like that. I'll let you borrow the money to pay your bill. Friday you can pay me back." That's sweet. "I can't let you do that. I'll be fine, it's only four more days." I tell her. "You are so stubborn, and you can't show up to work looking like this tomorrow. At least come stay at my place until Friday and your power is back on." She's right, I can't look and smell like this. "Fine as your boss, I'm ordering you to take the day off with me, with pay." I laugh a little, at least someone around here needs to get paid.

"Okay, let me get my things. Do you want to meet me there?" I shake my head. "Worst Uber ride in the history of all time. I'm not living through that again." I shudder thinking about it. "I'll drive, we can swing by your place to get your clothes." I'm so glad Sarah and I have been friends since college. I don't know what I would do without her.

Chapter Three

On the way, I tell her every bad thing that has happened today. After stopping at my place, we finally make it to Sarah's place in West Hollywood. Her parents are wealthy lawyers and bought her a condo as a college graduation present. It was either pay for college or a place to live. She chose this place. Now she doesn't have to worry about rent, just the yearly tax and HOA dues. She works because she has bills to pay and has to have money to eat.

"You should just move in with me. I have the spare room. You're more than welcome to use it. You would just have to pay for your food." This isn't the first time she has offered. "Sarah, I told you, we would get tired of seeing each other. All day at work and then you come home and see me again. It would ruin our friendship. But thanks for letting me crash here for a few days." She looks disappointed. "Just think of all the bills you could pay off, by living here. Just think about it, we can ride to work together tomorrow." She heads into her room and I head to my borrowed room.

The room is small but clean. The bed is made and there is a matching dresser and nightstand. I hang my clothes in the closet and unpack my bag. Across from me is a bathroom with a full-size tub-shower combo. I set my toiletries in there and a new set of clothes. Then turn on the water for the tub and pour in some lavender bubbles. I smell cigarette smoke as I pull my shirt over my head. Just great, now I'm going to have to spend more money to get these dry cleaned.

I step into the tub and let the hot water relax my muscles. The lavender smells nice, but my mind won't turn off. How am I going to handle a new client on top of the ones I already have? How can I continue to live like this? I need this promotion so bad. Maybe it isn't a terrible idea to move in with Sarah for a little while. I could get caught up on my bills and actually have money to fix my flat tire. With my mind made up I get out and get dressed. Then knock on Sarah's door.

"What's up, something else terrible happen?" She smirks. "No, I decided to move in with you." She screams and hugs me. "We have to celebrate! Let's go out!" I let her down easy. "I don't have the money to go out and celebrate. That's why I'm moving in with you and only for a few months. That way I can get caught up on my bills." She still looks excited. "It's my treat, just this once." She is so persistent. "I have work to do. If I don't help my new client's image, I won't have a job. Then you will be stuck with me forever." I joke, but I'm horrified at the thought. "I'll order in, do you want Chinese or Italian?" I shrug my shoulders and return to my room.

Once there I pick up the papers for my new client and get to work. Dr. Micah King age thirty-six, born in Australia and moved to the US at the age of twelve. He graduated from Harvard with honors in plastic surgery. Rated one of the top surgeons in Los Angeles last year, he built his practice from the ground up. For the last eight years he has worked on many A-listers in music, sports and the big screen. That all seems good, so why is someone suing him and slandering his name all over social media?

I shuffle through the papers and pull out the malpractice claim. One Katrina Thompson is suing Dr. King for breast augmentation. She claims her new breasts are uneven. Therefore, no one will hire her as an actress. I've never even heard of her. I pull up google and do a quick search on my laptop. After a few pages I think I have found her. She has starred in a few plays and some commercials on television. Never on the big screen doing movies or sitcoms.

While I'm there, I search Dr. Micah King. Immediately it pulls up the page for his practice. I click on it and it shows beautiful women and men in before and after pictures. I have to admit, he is very good. Me at a size nine; wouldn't mind getting a little tummy tuck. Once I click out of his practice page, I pull up a new article. It's a blog about how Dr. King mistreated Katrina and deliberately made her breast uneven. How he was rude to her and made it so she could never work in Hollywood again. What's wrong with her? Not every actress in Hollywood has to take her top off. There has to be something I'm missing. It doesn't seem like Dr. King would jeopardize his practice by deliberately messing up. I find his contact information and send out a quick email.

Dr. King,

I'm Anna Johnson, your new publicist from Image Inc. I would like to set up a meeting to discuss your case. Please email or call me at your earliest convenience.

*Sincerely,
Anna*

I leave my contact information at the bottom. Then start to reread the papers. I can't mess up; I need to know everything I can about Katrina Thompson and Dr. Micah King. My phone beeps with an incoming text.

Anna, This is Micah. I have an opening before my eleven o'clock surgery on Wednesday. Can you meet me at Cedars-Sinai hospital at ten am? I'll be in OR room five.

Wow that was quick. I leave my room, phone in hand to find Sarah. "Do you think I could borrow your car on Wednesday? I have a meeting with the new client at ten." She smirks. "I'm surprised you asked, are you sure you don't want to take another Uber?" That's why I love her, always messing with me. I send a text back to Dr. King, saying I'll be there. "No way in hell. When you get to work, I need you to find everything you can on Dr. King and the lady suing him. Something isn't right here, and I need to get to the bottom of it."

"Do you think she is just suing him for money?" Sarah asks me. "I don't know, and we can't jump to conclusions." There is a knock on the door, the food is here. Sarah pays and sets the food down. The smell of fettuccine alfredo makes my stomach growl. I feel bad that she is paying. But she knows I will pay her back. "I'll get on it, first thing in the morning. But right now, I'm hungry and my boss gave me the day off." We laugh and dig in. I hope my day

J. M. WILLIS

tomorrow, goes better than today.

Chapter Four

The drive from work to the hospital is only about ten miles. But ten miles in Los Angeles traffic, could turn into an hour of driving. Luckily, I arrive at nine-thirty. I park in the hospital parking garage and check my makeup. Then I reapply a little lipstick and walk inside. I'm not sure why I'm so self conscious right now. Maybe because Dr. King is a plastic surgeon and his job is to make everyone look perfect. I pull my pencil skirt down a little more as I make my way inside. My long brown hair is up in a twist and I look professional. Even my shoes match today. There is nothing else I can do now.

The signs are easy to follow inside and soon I'm standing in front of the operating room reception desk. "May I help you?" A lady in scrubs asks. "I'm here for a meeting with Dr. King, he is expecting me." I hand her my business card. "Yes Ms. Johnson, right this way. I'll take you to a private waiting area. He will be here as soon as he finishes this surgery." I follow her through some doors and turns. She leads me to a small room. "Just wait here, there should be coffee; if you're brave enough to drink it." With that she leaves me alone.

This must be a doctor's lounge. There are lockers that line one side of the wall. A couple of chairs and a small round table. The back counter has a coffee pot and cups. I sit at the table and pull out my laptop. The sign on the wall gives me the WIFI password and I pull up his case. I've already made a list of questions and possible things he can do to help his image. I'm reading my questions when a lady walks in. She looks worn out and goes right to the coffee pot. After she downs the scalding hot coffee, she throws her cup away and leaves the room without a backwards glance.

I look down at my watch, it's already been an hour. He must be caught up in surgery. I continue with my research. With everything in place, I even have time to check social media on my phone for Mia, my other client. The door swings open and a man in bloody scrubs rushes over to a locker. I can't see much of him with the surgical mask and cap on his head. His back is to me when he starts taking off the mask and cap. Then goes his scrub top. My eyes almost pop out of my head. This man's body is pure muscle, every inch of him.

I feel like a creeper, just sitting here ogling him. Maybe I should say something. He bends over as he slips off his pants. Now he stands there in only his boxer briefs. "Holy fuck." Slips out of my mouth, just as my phone falls to the ground making a loud noise. He turns around; as I stand to pick up my phone. I'm pretty sure my face goes red in embarrassment for being caught watching him undress.

Now that I see the front of him and his face, I can't speak. He looks me up and down. His blue eyes are in sharp contrast to his jet-black hair. This man is gorgeous. My heartbeat speeds up just looking at him. My eyes start to drift downwards and either he is huge, or he is very happy to see me. He makes a small noise. I quickly look up and see a cocky look on his face. He knows he looks good; I hate men who are cocky. Confident yes, cocky hell no.

"Sorry, I'll just turn around so you can finish changing." I turn around and lightly fan myself. "Don't turn around on my account, I don't mind if you watch." Wow, definitely cocky. "I'm sure you don't." I stay facing the coffee pot, hoping he hurries. "I haven't seen you here before. Are you a new doctor?" He asks, at least it sounds like he is putting on clothes. "No, I have a meeting with Dr. King. I'm sure he will be here soon." I explain why I'm in here.

"Dr. Micah King?" He asks me. "Yes, he'll be here soon. I don't think it will look good if he comes in here and you are undressed. It might give him the wrong impression." I say still facing the wall. No way I can look at that again, I might jump him. It's been over a year since I got laid and I might just say, screw this job and take him. "You can turn around, I'm dressed." I hesitantly turn around. He is dressed in a new set of green scrubs. "Well good luck. I have to go." He smiles and then heads out the door, leaving me breathless. I'm silently hoping he will come back and take me.

It's noon before anyone else enters the room I am in. It's the same lady that brought me here in the first place. "Dr. King sends his regards. He won't be able to make your meeting today. He would like to make it up to you, by buying you dinner. This is the address of the restaurant, he said be there at six." I take his business card; the address is on the back. "How will I recognize him? We have never met." She smirks. "Trust me you can't miss him." I gather my things and she leads me out to the front area and doesn't say anything else. All I can do is return to work and meet up with him later.

When I get back to work, I put the address into my phone. It's a trendy new restaurant in West Hollywood. Actually, it's walking distance from Sarah's condo. "How did it go Anna?" Sarah stands in the doorway. "He never showed, got caught up in surgery. We have a work meeting tonight at six. I can just walk there from your place." This piques her interest. "You mean your place. Remember you're moving in. Where is it?" I show her my phone. "I know that place, it's pricey, but the food is good." I pull open my desk drawer and grab a credit card I have hidden in there. "I'll just have to put it on the company card then, it is a work meeting." The rest of the day is uneventful and soon we make our way home.

"You are never going to believe what else happened to me today. I was in the doctor's lounge, waiting for him to meet me. Then another doctor came in distracted and just started undressing right in front of me. And let me tell you, I think my panties are still wet from that little strip tease. He stripped all the way down to his boxer briefs. Then I dropped my phone and he saw me there; I was just standing watching him. I've never been more embarrassed or turned on in my life. Every inch of him was perfect." I fan myself thinking about it him.

"What did he say when he saw you?" I smile remembering his cocky statement. "He said he didn't mind if I watched." Her eyes widen. "He did not. You are so lucky." She is delusional. "No way, he was way too cocky. Anyways, I have work to do before the meeting tonight. I'll see you later." She goes back to her desk and I'm stuck with my memories.

Chapter Five

Good thing I thought to pack a dress for going out. Otherwise I'd have to make a trip to my apartment and try and find something in the dark. I like to dress a little more casual than a business suit for dinner. It makes my clients relax and I can see how they really act. A lot of times they don't loosen up and they need to feel comfortable with me. I'm dressed in a little black dress with a green wrap. Green is my favorite color and it makes my green eyes stand out. If people are looking at my eyes, they aren't looking at my body.

I walk the short couple of blocks and I'm soon regretting it in these heels. My feet start to hurt, and I slow down. I'm only five minutes late when I walk inside. The guy at the podium greets me like I'm his new best friend. "Hey girl, aren't you looking good. Do you have a reservation?" He is obviously gay because he wears dramatic eye makeup and bright red lipstick. "I sure hope he made a reservation for us. Can you check for a Dr. Micah King? I don't know what he looks like." He looks at his list. "Yep, right here, six pm sharp. It doesn't look like he is here yet. Do you want to sit at the bar or your table?" I don't want to keep moving, my feet are killing me. "The table is fine, thank you."

"All right girl, right this way. My name is Honey, so blind date?" He asks as he takes me to a table and gives me a menu. "Thank you Honey, I'm Anna and no it's a business meeting. I hope he arrives soon, he stood me up earlier." Honey looks shocked. "Well he should be ashamed of himself; disappointing a lovely creature such as yourself. This is the wine list, the first one is on the house." I smile back at him.

"You don't know how bad I need that right now, thank you. I'll have the red wine. I don't care which one." Honey snaps his fingers in the air and my waiter hurries over. "Get my new friend Anna here a red, on the house. Well, I better get back, I'll bring him over when he gets here." I wave and he is gone. Soon the waiter arrives with my wine. Dr. King is now ten minutes late. My phone beeps.

Anna, my last patient took forever. I'll be there in about ten to fifteen minutes. Sorry, Micah.

Well at least he texted me this time. All I brought with me is a folder that fits in my oversized purse. I didn't want to deal with my laptop; I printed my list of questions. But I've already memorized them from waiting two hours earlier.

I'm sipping my wine and people watching when I see Honey again. He walks towards me and mouths "Oh my god," while he fans himself. I smile at him until he moves out of the way. Then I stare with my mouth hanging open. There is Dr. Sexy himself, the doctor from the hospital. Tonight, he has on suit pants and a white button up shirt, not scrubs. They stop at my table. Dr. Sexy holds out his hand to shake mine. "Anna, nice to meet you." I start coughing on my wine, this can't be happening. "No fucking way." Comes out of my mouth, the guy smirks at my outburst. Honey looks confused.

"Honey are you sure you have the right table?" He glances at Dr. Sexy. "He said his name was Micah King. Do you want me to check his ID?" I stare dumbfounded at Honey. The guy I guess Micah, takes out his wallet and passes me his driver's license. I pick it up, there is my proof. Micah King, organ donor stairs back at me in the picture. I slide it back across the table. "Thanks Honey, that will be all." He waits for a minute, looking back and forth between us, then decides to leave.

Micah sits across from me with a smirk on his beautiful face. "I can't believe you didn't tell me who you were earlier." I state, waiting for an explanation from him. "I can't believe you let me undress in front of you, without saying anything. Besides, I didn't want to cause you any more embarrassment." My face turns red. "Yeah well, you should look around the room to see if anyone is there, before you start stripping." His eyebrows shoot up. "I could strip for you again." What a cocky bastard.

"No thank you, I don't mix business with pleasure." I state, hoping he will drop it. He stares intently at me. "I thought you noticed; the pleasure was all mine." What? Oh my god, he is talking about his dick? My face goes even redder because he knows I was looking before. "Look Dr. King, I'm here to help your image in the community. It you can't keep it professional. I will have to assign you to someone else." I'm totally bluffing, but he doesn't know that. His intense blue eyes wander down to my chest, then back up to my eyes.

"Okay, if that is what you really want, let's start over. Please call me Micah, how can you help me?" Relief and an unexplained despair hit me at the same time. Then I remember my job is on the line and I can't afford to mess this up. "That would be best. I'm Anna Johnson, your publicist. You may call me Anna if you wish. I work for John Harrison II, the owner of Image. Our motto is 'Image Is Everything'. Could you tell me more about your relationship with Katrina Thompson? And why you think she is suing you for malpractice."

"That spiteful bitch is just mad because she can't make it to the big screen. Her breast came out perfect, they are not uneven." That's what I thought, but there are always two sides of a story. "Do you have before and after pictures?" He looks surprised. "Well not on me, I'm not a sick-o who carries around pictures of woman's breast." I laugh at that. "You have a beautiful smile Anna." I ignore his comment.

"I see your court date is in two weeks. I'm going to need to know if you had a relationship outside of work with Katrina. We don't need something biting us in the ass later." I wait for an answer. "We dated for a few months." And there it is, that's the reason she is suing him. "What did you do?" I ask him and he looks angry. "Why do you think I did something wrong?" Things are getting messy. "I'm not saying you did. Why don't you tell me about your relationship and why it ended?"

The waiter comes over and takes our orders and leaves to put it in. "Katrina seemed nice when I first met her at my office.

She is just like any other aspiring actress. She thought she wasn't being hired because her breasts were too small. Which is usually not the case here in Hollywood, unless you are going for adult films. It's not my job to judge people's decisions. I'm in this business to make money, not send it away. She had the money, so we set up an appointment. I make it a requirement for all of my patients to go to my counselor before surgery, it's included in the cost. That way all of my patients are informed of their options. Then they can make the right decision for their bodies. If they choose to not have surgery at that point, the counselor fee is waived.

Katrina went through the interview and I did her surgery. She went from a b-cup to a d-cup. The surgery went well and at her last follow up appointment, she asked me out. Since she wasn't my patient anymore, I agreed. We went out a few times, texted nothing serious. Then one day after a casting call; she started getting crazy. She started blaming me for her breasts being uneven. I told her I couldn't see her anymore and we parted ways. Four weeks later I got the papers, stating she was suing me for malpractice." I take a few notes.

"Did you sleep with her?" He looks at me in disbelief. "Why does that matter?" He asks. "Because if you went out on a few dates, that's fine. But if you slept with her and pictures start popping up of you and her in an intimate embrace. It makes my life more difficult. I'm trying to improve your image. I need to know how to spin this story to make you look like the good guy. If I know in advance, it is a possibility. I know which way to head." He leans back in his chair. "Then yes, I slept with her. Are you jealous?" This guy is so full of himself. I don't reply.

"I'm going to need copies of all of your text and emails. Any other correspondence between you two. Also, a list of all of the appointments she made, the ones she came into the office for. The dictation from the counselor interview, if you have it and yours too. Medical records from the hospital and the pictures. The places, dates and times you went out with her." I look up at him. He stares with his mouth open. "Are you my lawyer or my publicist?" He asks in disbelief. "I'm your publicist, is that going to be a problem?" He smirks. "No, I'll have my lawyer email you everything he has."

Our dinner is served, and we make small talk. "So, Anna, tell me about yourself." Micah asks. "I've worked at Image for the last four years. I graduated from UCLA with a bachelor's degree in public relations and I'm currently working on my masters." I tell him proud of my accomplishments.

"That's good, I like an ambitious woman. What part of town do you live in?" I try to keep it professional and not be rude at the same time. "I actually just moved close to here, I walked." This surprises him. "You live in West Hollywood?" He asks. "Yes, I moved in with my friend yesterday. So, you picked a good place to eat."

"So, Anna, is this new roommate a guy friend?" This man just doesn't stop. "Not that it is any of your business, but no, Sarah is a woman." I tell him. "And is Sarah your girlfriend?" His question confuses me. "What? Oh, of course she is a woman." I state. "You do live in West Hollywood." My eyes widen. Maybe I should just tell him she is my girlfriend; it might make him back down. But I don't like to lie to my clients.

"No just a friend. And before you ask, because I know you will. I don't have a boyfriend and I'm not looking for one. Let's keep this professional." He looks disappointed. I'm not sure if he is just a flirt or he is really interested in me. With the way he looks; he could have any beautiful woman in the world. Hell, he could do surgery and make them look beautiful.

The waiter returns with our check and I pull out the company credit card. But Micah beats me to it and hands his card over. "This is a business meeting; the company is happy to pay for dinner." I tell Micah. "I know, but I promised to make it up to you by buying you dinner. You did wait a long time in the doctors lounge." He states. I'm not going to argue with him. But I definitely already got paid with the strip show from earlier. "Well thank you. When do you think I will have all of the information I need?" I stand up and grab my purse.

Micah stands and we walk towards the front door. "You should have it in the morning." I wave bye to Honey as Micah opens the door. Honey fans himself again and I laugh. When I turn, I trip on a rug. Micah catches me. "Crap, I twisted my ankle." Micah picks me up, like I weigh nothing. "Put me down Micah, I can walk." He ignores my request and carries me a few feet over to a bench. Honey runs out, seeing me trip.

"Hey Anna, are you alright?" Honey asks me concerned. "I'm fine Honey, thanks for asking." Micah picks up my leg and starts to take my left shoe off. "What are you doing?" I ask as I try to pull my leg away. "Relax, I'm a doctor. Let me make sure nothing is broken." I stay still and let him examine my ankle. His big hands touch my ankle then slide up further. I get butterflies in my stomach from his touch. I try to hide it. But Honey is looking at me like he would do anything; to be in my shoes. I can feel the heat from his hands move up my body. Now I wish I could really go home for a cold shower.

Micah looks up at my face, frozen in place. His ice blue stare is intense. "It's not broken, just a sprain." He almost whispers. I snap out of it. "Great, I need to get home. Thank you for checking it out." I take my shoe back from him and slip it on. Then I stand and try to hide the pain it causes, because I have to get out of here fast. "I'll see you both later." Then I limp down the sidewalk.

"Anna wait, let me at least take you home. You can't walk all the way there." Micah states and I turn around. "Thanks, but I'll be okay." I tell him. "Just let him take you home, I would." Honey states as he gazes at Micah in lust. I'm going to regret this; I just know it. "Fine, but I'm walking to your car." He smiles and holds out his arm, for me to take. "Don't do anything I wouldn't." Honey yells out. I ignore his statement. I have no idea what he would or wouldn't do. We just met tonight.

Chapter Six

Luckily, we only have to walk a few steps to the valet. Micah smells too good and I'm standing way to close. My hormones are going into overdrive. He hands the guy his ticket and we wait a few minutes for his car. Soon a black BMW pulls up and Micah opens the door and helps me in. Then he tips the valet guy. I tell him my address and he punches it into his GPS.

I'm quiet as we make our way to my place. I silently give myself a pep talk. Don't do anything stupid Anna. You can't lose your dream job over some guy. Even if he is hot as hell and smells divine. "You're right you do live close; I almost wish it was further." We are parked outside of my new home for a few months. "Well thanks for the ride. I'll let you know if I need anything else." He opens his car door and hurries around to open my door. Then he offers me his hand as I get out. "Okay, bye."

I muster up all of my strength as I step away from him. You can do this Anna; I tell myself as I try not to limp. "Anna let me help you inside. I promise not to do anything." I stop in my pain of walking, tears threatening to spill over. "If you promise." He shuts and locks the car door. Then he is by my side. "Now don't argue with me. It will go quicker this way." I look at him questioningly. Then he bends down and picks me up again.

I have no words; I just try to hold by breath so I can make it through this. He carries me inside the building. "Which way?" I'm still trying to hold my breath, so I point to the elevator. His hands are full of me in them; I reach over and push the button. When it comes, I push the button for floor number three. The ride doesn't take long. Then we are heading to my apartment door.

When we get there, he lets go of my legs. But he is really tall, so I end up kind of sliding down his body. I feel every one of his amazing chest muscles. I think I've died and gone to heaven. I step back and get dizzy from holding my breath. I reach out to steady myself. My hand lands on a solid mass of chest. "Sorry." I apologize and try to step back. He takes the hand that was on his chest and kisses it. "Bye Anna." I stare at his ass as he walks away.

I open the door and limp inside. Then lean against the closed door. "Fuck!" I yell out in frustration. Sarah comes running, at my outburst. I slide down the door and land on my butt. "What's wrong?" Tears run down my face. "Anna, talk to me." I cover my face with my hands. "I'm going to lose my job; I can't work with Dr. King." Sarah sits on the floor in front of me. "Why, what did he do to you? I'll kick his ass if he hurt you." She says with a straight face.

I smile a little. "No, you don't have to kick his ass. I just can't stand to be in the same room as him. Do you remember the guy from the hospital? The one that stripped in front of me?" She nods yes. "Well that is indeed, Dr. Micah King and he is the biggest flirt I have ever met." Her eyes widen in shock. "How am I going to keep a professional relationship with him? When I can't stop thinking about his hot body? Do you know he actually carried me all the way up here to the door and kissed my hand." I explain. "Why did you let him carry you?" She asks confused. "I sprained my ankle. Can you get me some ice?"

Sarah heads to the kitchen to get ice for my ankle. I get up and wobble over to the couch. My phone beeps and I pull it out of my purse. It's a text from the man himself, with an attachment.

Anna, I hope your ankle heals quickly. My lawyer said he will send you everything in the morning. Sweet dreams. Micah.

I open the attachment. It's a picture of Micah standing in a pool of water. His white t-shirt soaking wet. His blue eyes stare back, mocking me. Almost as if he is saying, come and get me. My phone slips out of my hands. It crashes to the floor. Sarah rushes over.

"You dropped your phone." Sarah tries to hand me it; I can't make my muscles work. I just sit there in a stunned silence. "Anna?" She waves her hand in front of my face. "Anna!" She says more firmly. I mumble. "Text." She turns over my phone and reads the text. You can see the moment she opens the photo. Her eyes almost pop out of her head. "Holy fuck!" I nod in agreement. She sits, staring at the picture. The ice forgotten.

"You're in big trouble Anna. If he is sending you sexy pictures, he definitely wants more. You should just go to Mr. Harrison and tell him the situation. Then jump Dr. Hotty." I lightly smack her arm. "I can't do that. Mr. Harrison will fire me. This is my last chance. I can't let a guy stop me from my dream of being the newest executive at Image." I tell her. "Then you won't, try to keep your distance and communicate by text or email only. Don't reply to that text, just ignore it. You should probably delete the picture too. You know, avoid temptation." I glance at my phone, in Sarah's hand. "You're right, I'm going to grab that ice. Then go to bed and forget all about Dr. Micah King."

I pick up my discarded phone and limp to the kitchen. Then grab the half melted ice and make my way to my room. Once there I change into my pajamas and lay down. Then place the ice on my ankle. With nothing left to do. I pick up my phone and scroll through my emails. Nothing of importance, I delete most of them.

The texts are next, I click on Micah's. What does he mean by sweet dreams? Why did he send me this picture? I stare at it and can't believe how gorgeous he is. What is he doing flirting with me? He is probably just yanking my chain. My finger hovers over the delete button. But I can't bring myself to delete it. If I can't have the real thing, at least I have his picture to gaze at.

The more I stare, the more turned on I get. My body starts to heat up and tingle all over. I have to relieve myself. The pressure is too much. I slip my hand under my pajama bottoms and rub myself. He stares back at me in the picture. I'm so wet; just by looking at his picture. I remember his smell and his hands on me. It doesn't take long and I'm cuming. I throw the pillow over my head to block out my moan. Then jump in surprise when my phone beeps. The devil himself is texting me again. I hesitantly open it.

Anna, I hope it was as good for you, as it was for me. Micah.

No way, he can't know I just did that. There's no way. I search my phone frantically in case I dialed his number. There are no outgoing calls. It's not on speaker. I make up my mind right then. I have to avoid Micah King like the plague.

Chapter Seven

The next morning is Thursday, still one more day until payday. That means my car still has a flat tire. Good thing Sarah and I work at the same place. Otherwise I'd feel bad for her carting me around everywhere. I've decided to wear a pantsuit and low heels, to hide the ace bandage wrapped around my ankle. At least it feels better after the ice.

Sarah and I head inside and wait for the elevator. The people around us waiting keep giving me strange looks, it's making me self-conscious. I try to ignore them and stare at the door. But they keep whispering. Finally, the door dings and we step inside. I nudge Sarah to get her to look at everyone staring at me. She looks up from her phone, almost scared as she passes me her phone.

The headline for the article she is reading makes my heart race. 'Dr. Micah King Taken, Sorry ladies, looks like the hottest bachelor in LA has been scooped up by this dark haired beauty. We will be following this story closely. Everybody wants to know who has stolen Dr. Hotties heart.' There is a picture of Micah carrying me at the restaurant and another one in front of Sarah's condo. The last person gets off the elevator. "What the fuck! How did anyone even get these pictures? I'm going to be fired. I might as well just pack up my things right now." I say in a panic.

"No just go and explain what happened to Mr. Harrison. If he doesn't believe you, ask Micah to call him. It will be okay, I promise." Sarah's says trying to calm me down. "I don't think it will help, but I'll try." We get off on our floor and head to my office. My heart sinks when I see Mrs. Peterson sitting at Sarah's desk with a grim look. "Am I fired?" I ask her.

"The boss wants to see you now." I don't say anything, just hand my purse to Sarah and go back to the elevator, Mrs. Peterson follows me. At least I don't have to worry about rent, living at Sarah's. I'll have to skip classes in the fall, I won't be able to afford them. It will be okay. "Mrs. Peterson, it was nice knowing you. I always liked you." She just nods her head in agreement. We get off and she walks ahead of me and picks up her desk phone. "Ms. Johnson is here Sir." She sets it down. "You may go in." I take a deep breath and walk in.

Mr. Harrison sits calmly behind his desk. "Please shut the door Ms. Johnson and have a seat." I try to put on a brave face, as I do what he asks. Is this the calm before the storm? No way should he be acting so nice. He should be furious with me. After I sit, he speaks. "Do you like your job here at Image Ms. Johnson?" He asks me. "Of course, Sir, I love my job." I tell him truthfully. "So, would you say you would do anything to keep your job?" I might be able to keep it. "Yes Sir, anything." I answer a little too excited.

"I spoke with Micah King this morning. He explained why he

was carrying you. I hope your ankle is feeling better." I shake my head yes. "I have an ace bandage on it now, thank you Sir." I mumble out. "Unfortunately, the damage has already been done with the pictures. The press is having a field day. We need to nip this in the butt, and quick." He states. "I totally agree, we need to do damage control." He temples his hands, thinking.

"I have come up with an idea that I think will be beneficial for all of us. Dr. King is on board with the plan, all you have to do is agree." This is great, I get to keep my job. "Like I said, I'll do anything to keep my job. What did you have in mind?" He stares at me for a moment. "I need you to marry Micah King." My mouth hangs open. "What? I must have misheard you. Did you say marry Dr. Micah King?" He nods his head yes.

I stand up abruptly and start pacing. "Mr. Harrison, I'm not a prostitute. I can't marry him. We just met yesterday!" I yell. "I thought you said you would do anything to keep your job Ms. Johnson." He states. "Yeah, anything but that!" My face is red in anger. "Ms. Johnson, calm down, Micah agreed to this. I'm not asking you to sleep with him. What you do behind closed doors at his house, is between you two. I only care that you marry him and act like a loving supportive wife outside." He can't be serious.

"I have to live with him too! I don't know if I can do that Sir." His eyebrows draw together, mad. "Let me make this very clear then Ms. Johnson. You will marry Dr. King and move in with him by this weekend. If you don't, I will give this case to Becky. Then your career here at Image will be over. I'll give you until five tonight to decide. That will be all." He dismisses me.

I leave his office in tears. No, I'm not sad, I'm so pissed off. I don't even stop at Mrs. Peterson's desk, just hurry to the elevator. Sarah sees me in tears and follows me into my office. "I'm so sorry, you can stay with me as long as you need. Don't worry, you will find something else." She tries to encourage me. I point to the door. Sarah closes it. I open my mouth to tell her what happened, then shut it. How do I tell her what they want me to do? This can't be happening to me.

"I haven't lost my job yet. I have until five today to tell Mr. Harrison if I want to keep it." Sarah smiles big. "Why didn't you tell him already, of course you want to keep it." She says excited. "You don't know what he wants me to do, to keep it." I explain. "It doesn't matter, you love this job. You have to do it." Sure, like the decision is that easy.

"I wish it was that easy and I could just say yes. But I can't, I don't think I will be working here after five today. I should just start packing now." She stares at me confused. "But why? It can't be that bad." She tells me. "If I don't agree with Mr. Harrison's plan. He will give Dr. King's case to Becky. Becky, can you believe it!" Her face shows disgust.

"What plan? Just tell me already." Sarah complains. I wait, trying to get my words together. "By this Sunday, I have to be moved in and married to Micah King. If I don't, I'm fired." Her face is priceless. "Shut the fuck up!" She yells and I just nod my head yes. Sarah falls back in her chair, defeated. Well join the club.

"Don't tell me Dr. King agreed to this." Sarah states. "Apparently he is all on board. Mr. Harrison has already spoken with him about it." I don't believe he actually agreed with this crazy plan. "But you're not a prostitute." She complains. "That's exactly what I said. Mr. Harrison said I don't have to sleep with him. What we do behind closed doors is between us. But out in public, I have to act like a loving wife." Oh no, I know that look. Sarah is up to something.

"Would that be so bad? You don't have to have sex, just live with him and you can keep your job." I shake my head no in disbelief. "But he is the biggest flirt! How do I keep my hands off of him?" She smirks. "How long?" Huh? "How long do you have to stay married?" I shrug my shoulders. "I didn't ask."

Sarah gets up and picks up my desk phone. "Mrs. Peterson, could you tell us how long the contract between Anna and Dr. King would be in place." She pauses, listening. "Are you sure?" Another pause. "Okay I'll tell her, thank you." She hangs up with a smile. "Mrs. Peterson said six months and she also asked me to tell you. Micah King is so hot, she would do him, if she wasn't already happily married." I look up at my ceiling. "Why are you doing this to me?" I ask the lord up above. "Thanks Sarah, hold all of my calls. I need to be alone to think." Sarah looks sympathetic as she leaves and closes the door behind her.

I don't move from my desk. This is insane, I can't get married. No, I'll just have to find a new job. One where my boss doesn't ask me to put my reputation on the line. I'm not sure how long I have sat here with my thoughts; staring off into space. When my cell phone buzzes on my desk. I pick it up to distract myself. But fate has other plans, it's a text from Micah.

MICAH: *Anna, I'm sure you have a lot to think about. So, I'll make this short. I know you didn't want this, but I'm begging you to help me. You can have your own room and we don't have to sleep together. I'll be the perfect gentleman, I promise.*

I seriously doubt that. I text him back.

ANNA: *Micah, if you were a gentleman, you wouldn't have sent me a sexy picture of yourself last night.*

I push send. He texts back right away.

MICAH: *So, you think I'm sexy?*

Ugh, I can't believe him.

ANNA: *See, this is what I mean! Sorry but I can't do it.*

I send the text back pissed.

MICAH: *Sorry, I just can't help myself. I'm serious about my career though. If you don't want me to mess around with you I won't.*

I'm not sure about this guy.

ANNA: *How do I know if I can trust you?*

I wait a few minutes before he replies.

MICAH: *How about this? I won't touch you or do anything inappropriate in the next six months without your consent. If I do, I will have to pay all of your student loans off. But if you touch me first, all bets are off.*

That cocky bastard. No way would I jeopardize my loans being paid off.

ANNA: *Micah, you have a deal. When do you want to get married?*

His response is instantaneous.

MICAH: *TONIGHT!*

Oh my god, what have I gotten myself into?

Chapter Eight

I wait until the last possible moment to call Mrs. Peterson with my answer. Thinking I can somehow get out of this. But I'm still clueless and the clock reads four fifty-five. There is a knock, I know it's Sarah. "Come in Sarah." I tell her. She walks in wondering what I'm going to do. I might as well get this over with.

"I hope you are free tonight. Apparently, I'm getting married." She jumps and screams excited. "Yes! I knew you would do it. Did you tell Mr. Harrison yet?" The dreaded phone call. "I was just about to." I pick up the phone to call Mrs. Peterson. But set it down, when I see her standing in the doorway.

"I was just about to call you. I'll do it." She smirks at me. "Oh, I already know, Dr. King called me hours ago. I have everything set up. Are you ready to go?" Of course, he called her. "Um, go where?" Why does she look like she is ready to bust at the seams with excitement? "Just follow me. Bring your stuff." I pick up my purse and phone. Then follow her out. Sarah on our heels.

We get in the elevator, but instead of going down, we go up. Mrs. Peterson stays quiet as we go up one floor. We head down the hallway and stop in front of the bathroom. "Okay, everything you need is in there. I'll wait here, Sarah you go with her." I'm totally confused until I walk in the bathroom. There hanging up on the stall door; is a white wedding dress.

"Holy shit, this is happening, like right now." I say in a total panic. "Anna, you can do this. The sooner you are married, the sooner your six months will be up. Now, take your clothes off." She demands. I'm too stunned to do anything else. I take off my suit jacket, then my blouse and pants. Sarah helps me step into the beautiful gown. It's strapless and ties in the back. "You're going to have to take your bra off." She's right, it looks tacky. I take it off and Sarah does up the bodice. How did he even know my size? The dress fits perfectly. There is a box on the counter, I lift the lid.

Anna,
Thank you for agreeing to marry me. Even if it is only for a little while and it's not real. I'm sure your ankle still hurts, so I got you some flats to wear. Also, it would mean a lot to me if you would wear my grandma's pearl necklace. My grandfather dived in the Great Barrier Reef himself to find them. My mother would know this wedding is a sham, if you aren't wearing them.

Micah.

I pass Sarah the note and lift the tissue paper. The necklace is gorgeous and looks very delicate. I hand it to Sarah and turn around. She gently puts it on. Then I slip on the shoes and freshen up my makeup. I don't recognize the woman staring back at me. "Are you ready?" Sarah asks. "Hell no! But I agreed to this sham of a wedding, let's go." I try to sound confident, but inside I'm terrified.

Mrs. Peterson is still waiting for us. She smiles when she sees me. "Anna, you look beautiful." Are her eyes glossy? "Thank you, now what?" She leads us further down the hall to the stairwell. Then she heads up the stairs to the roof. I'm surprised when we step out to a garden terrace. Rows of greenery cover the whole roof. Twinkling lights hang from an arch in the middle. As we walk closer, I see Micah waiting for me in a black suit. Mr. Harrison stands chatting with him. Probably here to make sure I go through with it.

"Wow." Sarah states, staring at my future husband. I grab her hand for courage. We stop in front of them. "Anna, you look gorgeous. Thank you again." I nod my head, too nervous to speak. "Ms. Johnson, Grace and Sarah are here to be your witnesses. I was ordained today, and I will be performing the ceremony. We will take some pictures and they better be convincing." I nod that I'll behave.

"Okay let's get this over with. Ms. Johnson come hold Dr. King's hands. And dammit look lovingly at him, Grace?" She reaches into her purse and pulls out a camera. I tentatively take Micah's hands. How do you look lovingly at someone? I've never been in love. Micah smiles and I smile back. I see flashes from the camera. "Alright that's enough. Let's begin. Who has the rings?" Mr. Harrison takes a folded paper out from inside of his suit pocket. Mrs. Peterson passes me a gold band.

"We are gathered here tonight to witness the joining of

Anna Marie Johnson and Micah Elvis King." Sarah and I bust out laughing at the same moment. Mr. Harrison glares at me, I quiet down and look at Elvis the King, my future husband. "In holy matrimony. To have and to hold from this day forward. Do you Anna take this man to be your lawfully wedded husband?" Can I still say no? I squeak out my answer. "I do." I slide the ring on his finger, Micah smiles. "Do you Micah take this woman to be your lawfully wedded wife?" He doesn't hesitate. "I do." Is he excited about this? He slides my ring in place. "Then by the state of California, I now pronounce you husband and wife. You may kiss the bride."

"That wasn't part of the deal. Marry him, move in with him sure, but now I have to kiss him?" Mr. Harrison looks pissed, well get over it old man, so am I. "It's for the pictures Mrs. King. You know, seal the deal." He actually laughs at me. My boss, I didn't think he knew how to even smile. "Fine, Mrs. Peterson you better get this picture, because it is only happening once." I stare her down, she has her camera ready. As fast as I can I peck my husband on the lips. When I see a flash, I pull away.

"I'm straight and even I could kiss him better than that. You get over there right now and kiss him like he is the love of your life! If I'm not convinced, you're fired!" Mr. Harrison commands. I glance at my fake husband. "This doesn't count against the deal we made." I point to Mr. Harrison. "He is making me do this." Micah laughs at my situation. "We are still good." Micah tells me.

I slowly put my arms around his neck and lean in. He smells so good. Then I feel his hands slide around my waist. "Fuck it, let's do this." I kiss him, he kisses me back. Then his tongue slips into my mouth and he pulls me even closer. I feel every hard muscle of his lean body. Then I feel the hardness in between his legs. I lose control, I can't help it. Time ceases to exist. I don't know how long we have been kissing. One of us moans, I hope that wasn't me. I can't take this anymore. I pull away, stunned. Flashes bring me out of my daze.

"Was that convincing enough?" I say, so no one thinks I actually enjoyed that. "It will do. As a wedding present, I'm giving you tomorrow off, with pay. Spend that time to pack. I want you moved in together by Sunday. Congratulations Dr. and Mrs. King." Mr. Harrison leaves without a backwards glance. This is going to be the longest six months of my life. How am I going to keep my hands off of my sexy fake husband?

Chapter Nine

"Now what?" I ask to no one in particular. "We need a couple more pictures of you two facing the camera. In the morning there will be an article in the LA times. I booked the honeymoon suite at the Hilton in Santa Monica on the beach." Mrs. Peterson tells us. I think I'm going to pass out. "Honeymoon suite?" I whisper. Micah squeezes my hand. "For appearances only, don't worry I'll sleep on the couch." He tells me. "Then tomorrow, you start packing." She tells us and we pose for the last few pictures. Then we say our goodbyes.

This morning I woke up single, no boyfriend in sight. Now I'm married and we are headed to the Hilton, for our honeymoon. Well my husband better keep his hands off of me. Those wonderful, glorious hands attached to that perfect body. The ones that set me on fire. Fuck, I'm totally screwed. It takes about forty-five minutes to get there. Micah even rented a limo. I sit nervously in the back.

The car stops in front and the driver opens the door. Micah gets out and reaches for my hand to help me out. I don't even complain when he doesn't let go and we walk inside. We head over to check in. The lady behind the counter smiles big. "Congratulations! Are you here to check in?" She asks. "Dr. Micah King and my wife Anna King checking into the honeymoon suite." He tells her and pulls me closer. I smile playing my part in this sham.

She looks back and forth between us. "I thought I recognized you from your picture. It was all over the internet. Here is your key card, have a wonderful stay." She says. "Okay wife, I just love calling you that. Let's go have some fun." Micah says sweetly, I play along. "That's what I'm talking about husband." He picks me up in my wedding dress and carries me to the elevator. I giggle in delight, but what I really want to do is puke. People in love don't really act like this do they?

We ride all the way to the top. Then head to our room. He slides the key card into the slot. As soon as we are in the room, he sets me down. I scramble away from him. "That was torture. I hope you don't have to keep talking to me like some lovesick puppy." He just laughs at me and takes off his suit jacket.

"What do you want to do? How about room service?" Micah suggests. "That sounds good, I haven't eaten since this morning." He hands me a menu and I look at my options. "I'll have a cheeseburger and fries. Also, a diet coke and water. No wait, I need something stronger after today. The red wine sounds good." He smirks and takes the menu back. After a moment he calls and places our order.

"You should relax, think of tonight as a mini vacation. Go take a bath, get a massage or maybe sit in the hot tub." That does sound nice. "No, I can't. I don't have anything to change into." I now realize I will have to sleep in this wedding dress. And the day just keeps punching me in the gut.

"I had these sent up earlier." He holds up a plain shopping bag and sets it on the coffee table. "Sarah picked them out, you know, just in case you said yes." That little brat. I pull out a black sleep shirt, in bright red letters it reads 'Fuck It!'. I laugh and hold it up for Micah to see and he smiles. The next is a sundress, green with white flowers on the bottom hem. Then a black bikini. The last item turns my face the same red as the lace panties and matching bra. I shove them back in the bag.

"A massage sounds nice, but I need food first. Can you call and see if they have room for me? I'm going to change out of this dress." He is already on the phone. I pick up the green dress and head to the bathroom. No way am I walking around in a bikini. The honeymoon suite is really pretty. A king size bed dominates the room. There is a small table with two chairs by the balcony door, overlooking the ocean. There are pretty floral arrangements throughout the room. On the other side of the room is a loveseat, the coffee table separates it from two chairs. I stop in my tracks and look more closely.

"Um Micah, did you notice something missing in our room?" I say as calmly as I can, in my state of a total freak out. "I was wondering when you were going to notice." I'm pissed. "Where are you going to sleep? If there is no couch." I say louder than I intended. "I told you relax; I'll sleep on the floor." I turn in a huff and lock myself in the bathroom.

How do I make my client and now husband sleep on the floor? He's a doctor for god's sake. I'm shorter, maybe I can curl up on the loveseat. It's only one night. I reach behind me to pull the string of my corset and I yank on it trying to get it untied. It's not coming loose. With my back towards the mirror I see Sarah has tied it in a not. I try everything, but it won't come undone. "Fuck!" I say in defeat.

There is a knock on the door. "Everything okay in there?" Micah asks from the other side. "Yeah, I'm fine." I tell him, even though I can't get out of this stupid wedding dress. "Well the food is here, come eat." Just great, now I have to come out. I open the bathroom door and walk past him. He has the food all set up on the coffee table.

"I thought you were changing?" Micah asks me. "Don't even go there, let's eat." I'm starving. "Aren't you afraid you will get your dress dirty?" I look down, I didn't buy it. "Nope. It's not like I have to return it or that I will ever wear it again." I explain. He drops the subject and starts eating.

"I was able to get you set up for that massage. They can squeeze you in, in about an hour." He smirks. "Why is that funny?" I stop eating. "Well I don't think you are going to enjoy it." He states, trying not to laugh. "Why is that?" I glare at him. "Normally you have to get undressed to get a massage. And you seem to be too attached to that dress, to take it off." My face goes red. I throw one of my french fries at him. It bounces off his face and lands on his plate. He picks it up and eats it.

"You know for someone who graduated in public relations.

You sure aren't good at communicating." He says calmly as he eats. I stare at him. I know he is right and I'm acting like a child. I just don't want him to see me naked. "Fine, can you please undo this knot, so I can take this stupid dress off?" I say frustrated. He actually laughs at me. "Why didn't you just say so? Turn around, let's get this off." My face goes red embarrassed.

"You couldn't possibly do it without looking could you?" I ask sheepishly. His eyebrows shoot up. "I'm not Houdini. What's the big deal? He asks confused. "Because, I don't want you to see me naked." Duh, why else? "Anna, I'm a doctor, I see naked people all day long." He states. "Yeah but those people aren't your wife." He laughs. "You realize that makes no sense. Just turn around already so I can untie it, then I'll close my eyes; I promise." I reluctantly turn around.

"It really is in a knot. You would have never gotten it undone and you would be stuck in this dress forever," I feel him tugging. "There I got it. Do you want me to loosen it?" I step away. "No, I'm fine. Now close your eyes. I don't need you to see me naked." He closes them and I hurry towards the bathroom. "No fair, you've seen me naked." He yells, as I slam the door.

I'm finally out of this dress. I shove it on the ground and push it in the corner. I'm just standing there in my panties from this morning. I forgot I had to take my bra off earlier. I'll just put it on after my massage, no way am I going out there in a towel to get the bra from the bag. I slip on the green sundress and let my waist length hair down from the bun I had it in all day. Then use my fingers to comb through it. Maybe I can sleep in the tub and stay here all night. Crap, I can't do that.

I leave the bathroom and return to my half eaten food. Micah is sitting in the same place. His white button up is off and so are his shoes. Just his t-shirt and pants remain. His gaze follows my every move. "Stop staring, your making me self conscious." I complain and my face gets hot. "I'm going to take a shower. The spa will call you when they are ready for you to come down, it should be soon." He heads to the bathroom. "Okay."

The door shuts and I think of him stripping in front of me at the hospital. Quit it Anna, I reprimand myself. Stop thinking about your fake husband, you can't have him. The room phone startles me. I pick it up. "Mrs. King, we apologize for the inconvenience, our therapist had to go home sick. Could we possibly reschedule you to the morning?" It's not like I can argue, they were squeezing me in. "That's fine, I'll just cancel. We are checking out in the morning anyways." I tell them and hang up.

The shower turns on and I decide to put my sleep shirt on instead. Why wear the sundress it I'm just going to sleep? I change quickly before he comes out. Then grab a pillow and the top sheet from the bed. Might as well see if I can get comfortable on the loveseat. It's not so bad. After a few minutes; I hear a noise coming from the bathroom.

I get up to investigate. As I get closer, I realize it's moaning. But those aren't moans of pain. Oh my god, he is in there touching himself. "Anna, you're so beautiful." He whispers, then another moan. He is thinking about me? No way; another moan, longer. After a few minutes the shower turns off. I run back to the couch and get under the sheet. I quickly pick up my phone and scroll through it; trying to look innocent.

The door opens. I try not to look up, but the temptation is to much. Micah is only wearing a towel and he is dripping wet. He pauses when he sees me sitting there still. "I thought you went for your massage; didn't I hear the phone?" Yeah, I bet you did. "You did, they canceled. Someone went home sick." I try to keep a straight face; he looks a little startled. "Oh, that sucks. I'll get dressed." He picks up an overnight bag and returns to the bathroom.

A few minutes later he returns in boxer briefs. My eyes widen. "I thought you were getting dressed?" He looks down. "This is what I sleep in." This is going to be a long night. To avoid looking at him, I pretend to check my emails. "Here, you didn't drink your wine." He hands me my glass; I still don't look at him. I take the glass and down it in one chug. "Thirsty? You want me to have them send up more wine?" Why is he being so nice? "You aren't trying to get me drunk, are you?" I ask.

"You aren't trying to avoid looking at me, are you?" I look up, crap. My face heats up. "Nope, I'm going to bed, goodnight." I say in a rush. "Your sleeping on this?" He gestures to the loveseat. "Yep, the bed is all yours. Can you get the light?" I ask. "Well if you change your mind, I'll move." He walks towards the bed and I see his lovely ass. He turns off the lights and gets under the covers. After a little moving around he settles. I have a hard time getting my raging hormones in check. All I can think about is him touching himself and saying my name.

Chapter Ten

The next morning, I'm woken up by grunting. I open my eyes and look around. Micah is on the floor doing push-ups, in his boxers still. His body glistens with sweat. I watch for a minute, then feel guilty for spying on him. That is how I first met him. So, I get up and make my way towards the bathroom. "Sorry, did I wake you?" He asks, still working out. "No, it's fine, I have a lot to do today." I pick up my sundress.

"Do you want to eat before we leave? I can order room service again." I do need to eat. "Sure, anything is fine. I'm going to shower. Do you need the bathroom?" I ask him. Then I remember the shopping bag and pick it up. "No, I'm good." I shower and try not to think about what Micah was doing in here last night. How am I going to survive looking at his rock hard body for six months? I might need to stock up on batteries.

Once I'm done, I dress and put my hair up. I can already smell the bacon. This hotel sure has fast room service. "I'm glad you ordered bacon. Here, this belongs to you." I hand him the pearl necklace as I step out of the bathroom. "I ordered the same for me. How much stuff are you planning on packing or bringing?" He asks. "I haven't really had the chance to think about it. Clothes, shoes and maybe a few books. Not too much I'm only moving in for six months." I explain.

"Do you think you will need a moving truck? Or I have a pickup we can use." Of course, he does, and my one car is still stuck on the side of the road, with a flat tire. Thank goodness it is payday today. "If you can drop me off at my apartment, I can start packing. I only have a few things at Sarah's." I'm going to be packing for days. "Nonsense, I took the day off. My assistant rescheduled all of my patients. I can help you pack." That's nice of him. "If you're sure you don't have anything else to do." We finish eating and gather out things. I reluctantly pick up my wedding dress. It won't fit in the shopping bag, so I fold it in half and drape it over my arm.

"What's your address?" He asks as we walk out of the hotel. I'm surprised when his BMW is waiting for us at the valet. We came here in the limo. I tell him my address and he puts it in his phone. "What are you going to do with your apartment?" He asks, making conversation. "A lot has happened since Monday. My power got shut off and then my car broke down and I didn't have the money until today. I just decided to move in with Sarah, this week. That way I could pay my bills and continue to afford to go for my master's degree. I'm up for a promotion at work and Mr. Harrison said if I couldn't help you, he was going to let me go. Now we are married. I haven't had time to do or move anything but two suitcases to Sarah's. I just don't know. Fuck, my life is so complicated." I complain.

"I totally agree, your life is complicated. Let's uncomplicate it, how about this? When we get there, we can pack what you want to take. Then the rest we can put in storage for six months.

That way you don't have to keep up with the lease on your apartment." I do need to save money. "Sounds like a plan, I guess we will need a moving truck then. It won't fit in a pickup, unless you want to make multiple trips." We make small talk on the way; it doesn't take too long.

I'm surprised when we are driving down my street already. "Stop!" Micah screeches to a stop in alarm. "What's wrong?" He asks. "Mother fucker!" I yell and rush out of his car. "Anna, what are you doing?" Micah yells after me, I ignore him for a moment. Because a tow truck is trying to take my car. "Hey, wait that's my car!" The tow truck driver looks over at me probably thinking I'm a crazy person.

"Sorry Ma'am, someone called for a tow. Said this car has been here for a whole week. You'll have to get it from impound." He tells me. "I can pay you, how much?" He looks at my wallet as I pull it from my purse. "Do you take credit cards?" He smiles mischievously. "Cash only." Fuck the world, just what I need.

"How much?" I hear from behind me. "Two hundred." Micah pulls out his wallet. "No, that's way too much. You haven't even taken it anywhere. All you have to do is unhook it." Micah hands him the money. The guy smiles, since he practically robbed us and starts unhooking my car. "You shouldn't have paid him. It's way too much." I complain. "It would've been double that at the impound. Be happy we caught him now." I'm still angry when the tow truck leaves.

"So, besides the flat, what's wrong with it?" I glare at him. "Nothing." I state. "Do you have a spare?" I nod yes and he holds out his hand. "Keys." I hand them to him, and he opens the trunk. "What are you doing?" I ask confused to why he needs to get in my trunk. "I'm fixing your flat and before you yell at me again. Get over it, this is what husbands do for their wives." I stare dumbfounded. "But." That's all I get out before he gives me that look, like I dare you to say anything else. I stay quiet. If this is what husbands do; why didn't I get married sooner?

He is done, much quicker than I expected. He puts the flat tire in the trunk. "All done, you ready?" I'm not sure what to say. My fake husband just paid a guy two hundred dollars and fixed my tire. I kind of feel bad. "I hope you don't think I'm sleeping with you, just because you fixed my car." He laughs at my statement. "No way, you'll be the one seducing me." I flip him the bird, cocky bastard.

We get in our separate cars, for the one block drive. Then I lead him to my apartment. Two men stand outside my door, each with a stack of flat boxes. "Who the hell is that?" I ask and Micah smirks. "Thanks for getting here so fast. Is this all of them?" He speaks to the two guys. "Yeah, the packing tape is in the bags with labels. We can always bring more when we come back with the truck." He got a truck that fast? "I'll be in touch when I need you, thanks." Then he pulls out his wallet again and tips them. I stand there with my mouth open.

"Cat got your tongue? Finally have nothing to say?" He says as he uses my keys to unlock the front door. I follow him in. He turns on the lights. "Where do you want to start? I can start making boxes." My mouth is still hanging open. He looks at me questionly.

"Who the fuck are you?" I ask. "What, you don't know who

you married? That doesn't make you very smart." He says seriously. "Don't be a smartass. What the hell is going on here?" I ask again. "We are packing your stuff, so you can move in with me." He explains.

"Micah! Explain, now." I yell in frustration. "Oh, so you do know who you married." He tries to hold in a smile. I reach for the closest pillow on the couch and chuck it at him. It hits him in the face. "You really shouldn't have done that." He says sternly. He picks up three pillows at once and starts chucking them at me. I scream and run away. One hits me in the back, I duck and throw it back. I totally miss him, but he gets my head. "Enough!" I yell in a laugh. "Are you going to stop throwing things at me?" I smirk. "Maybe." I tell him. Then he slowly sets down the pillow he was aiming at me.

"Alright, I'll quit for now. My office manager set this all up. I just sent her a text with your address and what I needed. She is quite efficient." Wow, that was fast. "What about the power that is now on?" I have a sinking feeling. "My assistant took care of that too." He says as I get angrier. "I'm not some charity case! You don't have to go around paying all of my bills. We aren't really married." I object, he can't keep doing this.

"I don't mind, it wasn't that much." I glare at him. "Micah, while it was really nice of you to do. I'll pay you back. I don't want your money." Why doesn't he get that? "It's not like I can't afford it." Oh my god! "That's totally beside the point. I don't care how much money you have. You don't need to spend it on me!" He looks surprised. "Let's just start packing, you make the boxes." I'm done with this conversation. If he thinks he can just come in here and take charge, he has another thing coming.

It takes all day to pack the things I need to take. By the end it's only about ten boxes. "I'm tired, why don't you go home. I'll rest and then pack more in the morning." I need some breathing room. "Do you think it is wise to sleep under different roofs? We did just get married yesterday." Dam, he is right. "Fine, which house are we sleeping at then? Actually, I don't even know where you live." It's kind of strange not knowing where you are going to be living in less than two days. "Don't worry I don't live in the ghetto. If we use both cars, we can probably fit all of the boxes you are taking." I eye the boxes skeptically. "I guess I can start unpacking at your house then."

Chapter Eleven

We somehow manage to get all of the boxes in both of our cars. I follow Micah in my car to his place. Which for the next six months will be mine too. I can't believe I let my boss talk me into this. I'm so deep in thought thinking and following Micah that I just now realize where we are. Of course, he lives in Beverly Hills; I mean why not.

He pulls up to an iron gate that automatically opens. I follow him through to a crescent shaped driveway. Palm trees, neatly trimmed hedges and flowers are everywhere. The traditional style house is massive, two stories and at least sixty feet long. He stops in front of the house and gets out, then opens my door.

"Welcome home." He smiles proudly. "This is your house? It's beautiful and big, really big." I say in awe. "It's one of the smaller ones on this street. But it's home. Come on, let's get these inside." I grab one box and follow him in. "I'll give you a tour, just set that down." I do as he asks.

Everything is in pristine shape. Not of speck of dust to be seen. Fancy pictures hang on the walls. "This is the entryway and this set of stairs leads to the master bedroom and three other bedrooms. This is the living room and dining room." It must take an army to clean all of this. "Through here is the kitchen; outside is a pool and spa." He flips the lights on, and the pool lights up. "This remote controls the temperatures for both." I'm never going to want to leave, I think to myself.

"There is a small shower and bathroom in the pool house. I try to change out there, so Nancy doesn't get pissed off. Don't get her floor dirty, or you'll regret it." I stare blankly at him. "Nancy, my housekeeper; I would be lost without her. I'm sure she is around somewhere." I feel a sudden surge of jealousy. It comes out of nowhere. Don't be ridiculous Anna, Micah doesn't belong to you. Who cares If he sleeps with his housekeeper. It's none of your business Anna. I tell myself.

"There is another bathroom down this hall." We walk a little further. He turns on a light. "This is one of my favorite rooms. My office and the library." The whole back wall is made of glass, natural light streams through. A pretty garden with flowers, a fountain in the middle and a sitting area are outside. One side of the room is his office with a desk. But the other two from floor to ceiling, is a built-in bookcase. Every spot is filled with books. There is a seating area with comfy chairs.

"Wow, I love it." I can just imagine this room on a rainy day. Relaxing on the chase lounge, with a good book. It would be heaven. I follow him out. "In here is the living room." A big screen TV dominates the room, there are bookcases with DVD's. We stop at another set of stairs that lead down.

"And this is my bat cave." He says excited. We go downstairs to his bat cave, whatever that means. Probably full of video games. It's not, it is a full size gym. Every machine and weights set available. I look around in awe. One side of the room even has a hot tub. "What is this twenty-four hour fitness or something?" No way should one person, need this much exercise equipment.

"I take pride in my appearance. The better I look, the more my patients will want to do plastic surgery with me. It's all about business. I exercise a lot, to stay in shape. I'm not saying you need it, but say you came in wanting to change something. Are you more likely to do surgery with someone who looks like me or a fat guy?" I think about it.

"Neither, I would go with the surgeon with the most experience." I tell him. "Then you are one of the smart ones. Most people see me and think about the way I look." I roll my eyes at him. "Would you let me finish. They think about how society thinks you should look. The size one waist, with the big breast. The perfect nose or whatever it is. I'm one of the top plastic surgeons because people want to look like me. They have no idea; I have to work out a few times a day to stay in shape. All they care about is the quick fix, surgery will give them." I have no idea what to say about that. Maybe I was wrong about him. "Well keep up the good work, I guess. How many more rooms are there in this house? We still need to bring in the boxes."

We walk up to the main level and grab the boxes that we left at the bottom of the stairs. Then head upstairs to the second floor. "Those double doors to the right is my room. You can choose any of the other three on the left. Don't worry about Nancy. She lives in the casita over the garage." My eyes widen. "Your housekeeper lives with you?" I hope I don't have to see the two of them together. The thought makes me nauseous.

Micah looks strangely at me. "She lives in the casita, not with me and I need her close by." I stare at him, waiting for him to explain. "I told you, I would be lost without her. I'm not a messy man. But a house this big gets dirty. She also does all of the laundry and runs errands sometimes. I'll admit it, I'm a great surgeon, but I'm a terrible cook." I smile. "Finally, something Dr. Perfect isn't good at." I joke with him.

"I'm not perfect, far from it. But I know I look good. That's nothing to be ashamed of." He tells me. "You're still a cocky bastard. But you are alright. Which bedroom has a bathroom closest to it?" I ask, the closer the better. "The one next to mine has its own full bathroom. The other two have a bathroom in the middle of them." That makes it hard to decide. Be in the room closer with a bathroom or have to leave my room to use it. Then he might see me in my night clothes.

"I'll take the one with the bathroom." He leads the way and sets the boxes down by the closet. "Just start unpacking, I'll get the rest." He leaves me too fast to stop him. The room kind of looks like our suite last night. A king size bed, a love seat and coffee table. But instead of a table and two chairs there is a small desk. The bathroom has a tub and separate shower. Everything is nicely decorated and clean. I sit on the bed and take down my hair. Then take off my left shoe, my ankle is still sore from two days ago. I take off the ace bandage and rub it as I lay back on the bed. It's been a whirlwind of a week and I'm so exhausted; I fall asleep.

Chapter Twelve

I wake up disoriented. I'm lying on a bed in a strange room. There is a blanket covering me. How did I get here? Then I remember, I'm married, and this is Micah's house. It's dark outside; I must have been really tired. I don't even remember covering up and lying down. There it is again, the noise that woke me up.

I walk over to the bedroom door and hear arguing. I can't see anyone with the door closed and I can't open it without them noticing. "Micah, who is this woman?" There is a pause. "She is my wife, didn't you read the paper?" I forgot about that; the article should have been in there this morning. "That doesn't explain anything. I didn't even know you were dating anyone." She says angry. "Well it all happened pretty quick. I just knew I had to marry her as soon as I met her." He explains.

"What is it then? Does she want your money or is she pregnant? That is the only reason someone gets married this quick." She practically yells at him. "I know, I'm sorry I didn't tell you." Who is this woman he is apologizing to? "Sorry isn't going to make this better Micah. You better start explaining right now!" I'm about to open the door and intervene, when Micah speaks again. "Mum, I love her! I shouldn't have to explain anything else. I'm a grown man, not a child." What? My heart flutters. Don't be ridiculous Anna. He is just saying that to get his mother off of his back. What is wrong with me?

"You can't fall in love this quick. How long have you known her?" We should have made up some story of how we met. "She is my publicist, not some stranger I met on the street." There is a pause. "Well I want to meet her, where is she?" Crap, I so don't want to deal with this right now. "Another time mum, Anna is sleeping right now. We have been packing all day. How about you come back on Sunday for dinner?" Please say yes. "Fine, but I want details. I can't believe you didn't invite your own mum to your wedding." She protests. "Mum, we eloped. Anna didn't want me to waste my money on a big wedding. Trust me you will love her as much as I do. But not until you meet her on Sunday. Now goodbye, I need to sleep."

It's quiet for a few minutes. Then I hear the front door shut and then a light tap on my door. I contemplate even opening it. But decide to anyways. Micah stands on the other side, in pajama bottoms and a t-shirt. I'm almost disappointed to not see him in just his boxers. "Sorry about that, I guess you heard all of that." Why is he saying sorry? "She was pretty upset with you. We need to come up with something better than me being your publicist. She said she wants details." Micah looks strangely at me.

"What's wrong?" I ask him as he stares at me. "Anna, you are so beautiful. I like it when you wear your hair down." I stare dumbfounded. Then I look down at my wrinkled sundress and tangled hair. "Stop messing around, your mom will be back in two days. We have to come up with something." Even if I can't think straight with the way he looks at me.

"You know, I've only lied once to my mum before. I told her the truth; you are my publicist. We don't need any details. She will know if I am lying." I'm starting to panic. "If we can't even convince your mom, what are we going to do then?" Micah smiles mischievously.

"It's simple, we don't lie." Huh? "I don't know what planet you are living on, but shit is complicated. And we are right in the middle of a big pile of it." He laughs at me. "You worry so much, I have a plan." He tells me. "Yeah and what is your plan?" Too quick to step back, he grabs be by the waist and kisses me. I kiss him back, because who am I kidding, I can't resist. His hands are all over me. I feel him pull lightly on my hair. My heart beats a mile a minute. Micah is kissing me because he wants to; not because my boss told him to. Things are heating up too fast. He slides his hand down my leg and starts to pull my dress up. Reality sets in and I forcefully push him away.

"Micah, what the fuck?" My breathing is rapid, and my panties are wet. I try to calm myself as I stare at him. The hottest man I've ever met, stares back in lust. Definitely turned on by the way his pants tent out. How can he be turned on by me? "Sorry, I couldn't help myself." I glare at him, to shaken up to say anything. "Anna, are you mad at me?" He asks concerned.

"I'm fucking furious!" I yell at him. He hangs his head in shame. "I'm sorry, I guess I'll leave you alone." He turns around and heads towards his room. Now I feel bad, crap I have to come clean. "Micah, wait." He turns around. "I'm not furious with you. I'm mad at myself." He looks confused. "Why, I'm the one that kissed you?" Now I hang my head.

"Anna?" His voice seems closer. I look up at those ice blue eyes. "Why?" Is all that comes out of my mouth. "Why what?" He asks. Come on Anna, you can do this, just tell him. "Why do you want to be with me, when you can have any beautiful size two women you want?" He looks shocked.

"Anna, you are gorgeous. You have the perfect hourglass figure. Most of those women are fake as hell and I made them that way. They are conceited and full of themselves." He can't be serious. "I don't believe you." He tentatively takes my hand, I let him. He pulls my hand closer, right on top of his still hard dick. "Does this feel fake?" My face goes red and I quickly pull away.

"Well I can't sleep with you." I reluctantly tell him. "Okay, I'll back off, if you tell me why not." He stands his ground. "Because I'm not a prostitute. You made the first move, so you have to pay my student loans. That was the deal we made. It would feel like I had sex with you, just so you would pay them, it's not right." I protest.

Micah laughs and pulls me close. I try to pull away, but he holds on. "Anna, I already paid off your loans. And I didn't do it because I thought you would sleep with me. I did it as a thank you; for getting me out of this mess." This time he lets me go, when I pull away. I start pacing, I'm so confused. I do a quick calculation in my head. The two hundred for my car, the money for the moving company and my power bill. Now my student loans. I stop in my tracks. "Micah, that had to be over forty thousand dollars. You don't thank someone with that kind of money! You say thank you or you send flowers." I try to explain to him.

"Anna, it's not a big deal." Is he crazy? "Forty thousand dollars is a big fucking deal!" I yell back. "Come on, I want to show you something." He pauses at the stairs, waiting for me to follow. "You better not be taking me to the red room of pain." He shakes his head. "You watch too many movies. I'm not Christian Grey and I don't have a playroom." He leads me to the library downstairs. "Too bad." I smirk as I pass him. He smacks my ass and I yelp in surprise.

"I was just kidding, I'm not into S and M." He walks over to his desk and punches in a few keys on his laptop. "Just get your fine ass over here." I hesitantly walk closer to him. "Come on, I won't bite, unless you want me to." He teases me. I glance at the computer screen. "What am I looking at?" Micah stands behind me, a little too close. He whispers in my ear. "It's my bank account." I don't care what it is at this point. I close my eyes as goosebumps race down my arms and legs. I shiver and rub my arms.

"Anna?" I can't even think straight, with him standing so close. "Yeah?" He places his hands on my waist and gently pulls me closer to him. His arms incircle me and he kisses my neck. I feel him hard behind me and I moan softly. He continues to kiss my neck, driving me crazy. Then he slowly moves his hands up to my chest and squeezes lightly. My nipples are so hard they almost hurt.

"Anna, let me have you just once. So, I can die a happy man." He whispers seductively turning me on even more. I can't take it anymore; I turn around and kiss him. The laptop forgotten; I pull at his shirt trying to get it off. My moves frantic now that I've made up my mind. Micah lifts me onto his desk and steps back to take it off. His pajama bottoms are next, only his boxers stay.

He moves in and pulls my dress over my head, in one swift movement. I look down, my long brown hair hangs down to my waist. I'm wearing the red lace panties and bra Sarah bought for me. I try to cover up by holding my arms across my body, embarrassed. "Don't, you're beautiful." He pulls my arms away as he kisses me. I'm too lost to care anymore.

I might cum just by him kissing me. It's been way too long. I've never felt so turned on and he hasn't even touched me there yet. He reaches behind me and my bra slides down my arms. I hold it close, almost on instinct. But he starts moving his kisses down to my breasts. I let it fall to the floor. He sucks my nipple into his mouth. It tingles all the way to my core. My breath hitches and I grip the desk.

It doesn't take long until he moves further down. I clamp my legs shut fast. "Anna, come on let me taste you." His blue eyes plead with me. "No way. I haven't showered since this morning at the hotel. We've been working all day, I'm not clean." I complain and he smiles wide.

Micah stands and I stare in lust. God he is gorgeous, I can't keep my eyes off of him. Muscles define every inch of him. In one quick move he lifts me off the desk and throws me over his shoulder. "Micah, what are you doing? Put me down!" I shriek in surprise. He smacks my ass. "Be quiet, or I'll do that again." He carries me out of the library. I squirm trying to get free. He smacks me again. "Stop moving around." It is hard to stay still when you are topless and only in your panties, thrown over a man's shoulder.

At the top of the stairs he heads to his room. I can't really see anything but his glorious ass. He stops and opens a door. Then I hear the water turn on. He steps inside and I scream; expecting it to be cold. Another slap on my ass. "I told you to be quiet. Don't worry the water is warm." I slide down his body. Then I hear a rip as he tears my panties off. I stand before him naked as the day I came into this world. And I try to keep my arms down and not cover up. Micah stares hungry like a man starved, water running down his body. He steps closer and I back up, a little intimidated. My back touches the shower wall.

"You have no were to run to little Anna." I gulp and stay still. "Anna, tell me you want this as much as me. If you don't, I need to know, right now. Because in about three seconds there is no turning back. You will be mine." Holy crap, I'd have to be insane to walk away from him now. "I want you." I say clearly.

Then he is on me. His hands so warm and strong. He pulls me close and then we are both under the water spray. My hands roam and I tug on his wet boxers. I need to touch him. He pulls away but doesn't take them off, he reaches for the soap instead. I pout as he squirts some soap into his hands. "Not yet." He says, but I'm not disappointed for long. He rubs the soap over my breast, then my stomach. I hold my breath as he finally touches me where I need him the most.

He kisses me and his fingers feel so good. I moan as he rubs right over my clit. He doesn't let up and soon I'm panting. "Micah don't stop." He puts a little more pressure and I'm flying over the edge. "Fuck." I say as I cum hard. Micah smirks at my outburst. Then licks his fingers. "If you don't fuck me right now, I might die." He tells me. "Me too." I tell him honestly.

Micah pushes me against the shower wall and devours me. Then he lifts my leg. I can't get close enough. The pressure is building again fast. I wrap both of my legs around him and rub myself on his hardness. I cry out in frustration, because his boxers are still on. "Micah, please." He turns off the water and steps out of the shower. Then he sets me on his bed.

"Hurry up, take them off. I need you inside of me now." He bends down as he peels them off. Then he throws them somewhere in the direction of the bathroom. I have no idea where they land because I can't take my eyes off of his cock. "Holy fuck, do you think it will fit?" I ask in awe. He just smiles and kisses me softly. "Lay back." He whispers in my ear. I do as he asks.

He starts from the bottom and kisses up my legs. I tremble in desire. With each kiss my heart beats faster. He pauses and gently moves my legs apart. "Micah do that later. I need you now." I say desperately. Then his tongue touches me, and I can't speak anymore. He sucks on my clit and slides his finger inside. I lose all train of thought. All I can do is feel.

What is he doing, that feels so good? It's never felt like this before. I look down at him and I'm surprised to see blue eyes staring back at me. Now I can't look away. His gaze doesn't break as he licks and sucks. I don't look away until my eyes roll back in my head as I cum. Then he is on top of me. He kisses me and I can taste myself on his lips. I'm so turned on; I'm not thinking straight. Good thing one of us is. Micah reaches over to his nightstand drawer and grabs a condom.

I take it from him and slide it on. My hand doesn't reach all the way around him. I stroke him a couple of times. But I can't wait any longer. I lay back and he moves closer. He is just barely touching my entrance, with the tip of his cock. "Anna, are you sure? We can stop now." That's sweet, giving me a chance to change my mind. "No fucking way." In one fast moment he slides all the way in, leaving me breathless. "Fuck, do that again." It's almost too much, but I don't want him to stop. He does it again and again.

"Anna, you feel so good." I wrap my legs around him. The angle hits me just right and I'm going to cum again. "Micah, fuck." I say and he keeps going. I'm not sure I can take much more. "Anna look at me. I want to see your eyes as you cum again." He stares intently. "No, I can't cum again. It's too much." I tell him desperately. "Wanna bet?" He smirks and kisses my neck. Who is this guy and where has he been all my life?

Each thrust hits me right where I need it. I don't know how it happens, but my body heats up again. Like it can't get enough. I moan and close my eyes, almost there. "Anna?" I open my eyes. Then I'm lost in the blue ocean, Micah stares back in lust. I try to look away and he slows down. When I look back, he starts again. Making sure I look at him. This endless pounding is driving me crazy. His eyes entrap me as I cum harder than the first two times. Just as I'm about to shout out some profanity, he kisses me hard.

My whole body shakes in release. I feel Micah cum too. His breathing rapid, he collapses next to me.

"What the fuck was that?" I say in disbelief. No one has made me cum three times. It's hard to get just one out of me. "I'm just getting started. Give me thirty minutes and some water." He tells me. "You have got to be kidding me. I can't, not tonight." I say in a yawn and sit up to go to my own room. "Don't go." He pulls me close. "Micah, I'm too tired for more sex." Even I can't believe I'm saying this. "Okay just sleep. You feel too good to let you go." I'm too tired to move or argue. I lay my head down and promptly pass out.

Chapter Thirteen

The light shining through the windows wakes me the next morning. Regret sets in quickly as I think about last night. I can't believe I slept with Micah. Even if it was the best night of my life. It can't happen again. I'm here to work on his image, not sleep with my fake husband. This wasn't supposed to happen. How am I going to last six more months?

I glance over towards Micah's side of the bed. I'm disappointed he is not there. What is wrong with me? I just decided not to sleep with him again, now I miss his body. Fuck, this is going to be a long six months of torture. How can I keep my hands off of my husband; now that I've had a taste of his glorious body. I'm totally screwed.

Well I have to get up and face him. Might as well get it over with. I sit up and pull the blanket to cover me. It's then I see a robe at the end of the bed, a note on top.

Anna,

I hope you know; I'm never letting you slip away; not after last night. I had to run some errands. Be back soon. You better be ready for round two.

Micah

I stare at the note, in total shock. What am I going to do? I have to get out of here. His smell is filling my lungs. Even though he isn't here, I'm getting turned on. In a panic I grab the robe and throw it on as I race out of his room. As soon as I get to my room, I start pulling things out of boxes looking for my panties and bras. No way am I going downstairs to get my bra from the library. And my panties are probably still in shreds in his bathroom. I wonder how his maid will feel about that?

This is insane, I shouldn't care what his maid thinks. It shouldn't matter if he sleeps with her or not either. But I do care, and it pisses me off. I have no claim on Micah. He is free to sleep around. No fuck that, he married me. Not for real, but I'm not letting him ruin my reputation too. When he gets back, we are going to have a long talk. He better agree, or this shit is over. I won't even move in, screw Mr. Harrison and his job.

With my mind made up and my clothes on, I grab my purse and keys to leave. I head downstairs and, in my haste, I run into someone. I didn't see her because she was bending over. She scrambles to get up. "Who the fuck are you?" I stare her down. "I'm Nancy, Micah's housekeeper." Yep, the perfect slim waist and big breasts. He is definitely sleeping with this hot little Latino number.

"Well, I don't know what was going on here before. But keep

your hands off of my husband, he is mine now." I demand. She puts on a good innocent act, but I can see right through her. "Mrs. King, it is not like that. I have never slept with Micah." This pisses me off even more. She is the help; shouldn't she call him Mr. King? She is calling me Mrs. King. "Whatever, I don't want to know. Please tell Mr. King I went to my apartment to pack." I don't wait for an answer. I have to get out of here and maybe to the nearest bar. So, I can drink the memories of last night, right out of me.

I start to calm down as I drive towards my apartment. Then the tears start to fall, this is all too much. What is wrong with me? I shouldn't have yelled at Nancy. I just met Micah four days ago. I shouldn't have any reason to be jealous of his maid or anyone else. Micah is not mine; I'm just borrowing him for six months. Then we will get a divorce and go our separate ways.

I decide not to go to the bar. Drinking isn't going to get him out of my mind. Anna, Micah is not yours. Maybe if I repeat that enough, it will sink in. I pull into my spot at my apartment. Then check my face in the mirror. Crap, I look horrible. Mascara and eyeliner run down my face, the tears making it worse. Now my eyes are red and puffy. I use a tissue to clean up and a hair tie to put my hair up. I'll shower when I get inside, this will have to do for now.

As I walk inside, I stop when I see a familiar car; a black BMW. Why would Micah be at my apartment? I hurry inside and head upstairs. My apartment door is wide open, and I hear people talking. "Be careful with that, I don't want anything broken. My wife would be pissed, trust me when I say you don't want to piss her off." I stare with my mouth hanging open. Three men and Micah are busy packing all of my stuff. One wall is lined with neatly stacked boxes. All labeled with the items inside. The furniture is all gone, nowhere in sight.

How did they get so much done? I look down at my watch, it's only nine in the morning. "Micah?" Is all I can get out. He looks up from a box he is packing. A huge smile spreads across his face. "Anna, you're here." He rushes over and gathers me into his arms. I play along because people are here. He briefly kisses my lips, but I turn my head away from him. "Sorry I forgot to brush my teeth." He laughs. "I don't mind." I pull away.

"What is going on?" I gesture to my almost packed apartment. "We got a head start. I didn't want you to have to pack all weekend. You've had enough on your plate." I look around in a daze. Then the tears come again, I try to hold them back, but I can't. Micah pulls me close and I drop my purse. "Could you guys take a break? I'll call you when I need you." He reaches into his pocket and gives the movers some money. They take it and the three of them leave. The door shuts behind them.

I don't know how long we stand there. Micah just holds me and rubs my back. Why is he being so nice to me? That's what I don't understand. We only met four days ago, and he has already done so much for me. I have no idea what to do now. My apartment is basically packed. I planned on packing all weekend, to get away from him. I guess I could get caught up on work, since I was forced to take two days off this week. I step back and wipe my face.

"Sorry, I don't know what happened. I think we need to talk." He seems concerned. "It's never good, when a woman says she wants to talk." He states. "You have to stop paying for things and doing everything for me. I'm a big girl, I can take care of myself. You don't owe me anything, we only met this week." I explain.

"I just wanted to make sure you got moved in, without causing you to have more stress. You know, uncomplicating things." Micah tells me. "Well things got a whole lot more complicated last night, when we slept together." He smiles and steps closer. "But that was a good complication. I think we should try for four tonight." My face turns red as it heats up. Micah kisses my neck, sending goosebumps down my arms.

"No, we can't sleep together again. We were supposed to keep things professional." I say as I step back. "It's a little late for that." I roll my eyes at him. "Look, I appreciate what you have done for me. But it needs to stop. No more paying my bills and paying people to pack my apartment. I could have done it myself and only paid for the moving truck. I don't want or need your money." I tell him truthfully.

"You're so sexy when you are mad." Ugh, really? "Micah, quit it. What's going to happen if we get in a fight in the next six months? I can't even move out until then. It's too much of a risk, I can't do it." I try to explain, men are impossible. "You wouldn't have to move out. I have a very big house. We might not even see each other." He laughs at his remark. "See this is what I mean! I've only been there one night, and you are already pissing me off." It's like talking to a wall. Nothing is getting through.

"Anna, it's going to be way harder living together, if I can't touch you. Just think about no sex for six months." He makes a valid point. "I can't be your fuck buddy. Not without emotions getting involved. It's not fair to you or me. Especially when we get divorced in six months." I'm already jealous of the other women he is sleeping with. How will I be in six months?

"I have an idea." I roll my eyes at him again. "Your last idea was to sleep together." I state. "Just hear me out; six months is a long time. Last night was amazing and I'd be lying if I told you I didn't want you right now." I cross my arms over my chest. Hiding my suddenly hard nipples. "My point is, I don't think I can resist you. But I'm willing to back off a little, if you agree to date me." This man is crazy. "Let me get this straight, you want to date your wife; the one that you already live with? You know how insane that sounds don't you?"

"I'm saying I want to get to know you. See where this goes." I'm sure he does, all of me and in bed. "How would that even work? We go on a date and then we go home together. We will just end up in bed together again." I try not to picture him naked above me. "I'll try to resist you for a little while. Just give us a chance, you might be surprised." This is the worst idea. But we do have to live together. "Why not, but no sex." Little does he know it's not him, I'm worried about. I'm worried about me and my raging hormones. My fake husband knows exactly how to drive me wild.

Chapter Fourteen

The movers came back and finished packing up my apartment. Micah and I cleaned so I could get my deposit back. It's getting dark by the time we finish up. "How about we go home and change? Then I'll take you out to dinner. Think of it as a practice run before you meet my mum tomorrow." My eyes widen, remembering we still have to come up with a story of how we met.

"That's probably a good idea. We need to think of something to tell your mom. Also, we will be out in the public. I'm not sure how someone got those pictures of us. But I'm sure they are still out there waiting to strike again." Micah looks a little guilty. "Yeah sure, are you ready to go?"

"What aren't you telling me?" He better not lie to me. "It's nothing." I stare at him. His face is getting red and sweat starts to form on his forehead. "You wouldn't lie to your wife, would you?" He wipes his forehead. "You got me, I'm a terrible liar, that's why I can't lie to my mum. Just look at me." I smirk at Dr. Perfect, he's not so perfect anymore. "Well, what is it?" He takes a deep breath.

"My attorney spoke with the newspaper. The picture was sold to them." I figured as much. "Did they disclose who it was?" He glances at his feet and then looks at me head on. "It was Katrina." My mouth pops open, then closes. "What the fuck Micah? Where you just going to keep that a secret? I may be your wife, but I'm also your publicist. This is the woman suing you!" I yell at him.

"I was just trying to spare you for a few more days. At least until you were all moved in. You've been through a lot in the last week." I can't believe him. "Let me worry about me. Katrina is the reason we are in this mess to begin with. You can't keep things like this from me. Did you tell her we were going to that restaurant?"

"No, I swear I didn't tell her. I haven't spoken to her in two months." His face isn't red, and the sweat has stopped, he must be telling the truth. "Then that means either someone told her you were going to be there, or she has been following you." He doesn't look surprised. I stare at him waiting.

"Alright, I think she has been following me. I've seen her a few times around town. I didn't know she was at the restaurant that night though." I'm fuming by now. "Has she tried to talk to you?" Why would she follow him? "No, which is why I thought it was just a coincidence. That was until I heard from my attorney. If she sees us out together, maybe she will back off."

"Then let's go home and get ready for our date. We can put

on a show for the public and Katrina too. They won't know what hit them." Micah smiles big and steps forward, I back up. "No, I told you I'm not sleeping with you, I will date you. When we are in public you can touch me, but not when we are alone." But he licks his lips while staring at me. God help me, I can't help but shiver.

We take our separate cars home to get ready. I hope his ex-girlfriend isn't some psycho bitch. She is already suing him and now she might be stocking him. This is our first outing since we got married and I can't decide what to wear. Something comfortable or something sexy. Well if Katrina shows up, I want to at least look good. Yeah that's the reason; not because of Micah.

I come downstairs in a sexy little black dress. My make-up is done and my hair hangs in long silky waves. I tell myself I didn't wear it down for him. But who am I kidding, I gave him free rein to touch me in public. I'll show her who has Micah now. Even if it's only for a little while. And she better not touch him, he's mine.

"Wow Anna, you look gorgeous. Are you ready?" I pause to stare. Micah is wearing dress slacks and a white button up. He looks like a GQ model. "Thanks, where are we going?" I ask as we head outside, and he opens the door to his BMW. I slide in and wait for him, then we are off. "That depends, do you like to dance?"

We valet at a club in Los Angeles, the neon light flashing says Pearl's. There is a long line wrapping around the building. "How long do you think we will have to wait?" I ask him, but he doesn't answer. Instead he grabs my hand and pulls me towards the door. People in line yell for us to go to the back. Micah ignores them and leads us to the bouncer. The guy removes the velvet rope and lets us in, just like that. He didn't even speak to him.

As soon as we step inside the music is blasting. We head along the right side where it is less crowded. The dance floor can be seen below us, the bar is up ahead. The floor we entered through is where the tables are. We head towards a roped off section that has private booths with drapes, some are closed off. Another man stands guard.

"Micah, welcome back. I wasn't expecting you tonight." He must come here a lot. "Hey, Zack it's been awhile. This is my wife Anna." Zack smiles big. "Oh, I know, I read all about it in the paper, congratulations man." He gives a nod towards me. "You have a booth for me Zack?" He lifts the rope and leads us to a booth in the back. It's a red curved sofa with pillows. A small table in the middle. One of the drapes hangs loose and the other is tied back. I wait for Zack to leave to speak.

"So, is this a sex club or something? What's with the private booths?" I ask. Micah smirks and pushes a button on the wall. I stare at him, them jump in surprise. "What can I get you?" A voice says over the intercom. "We'll have the Pinot, Jack Daniels for myself and a platter please." He finishes with the order. I stand there with my hands on my hips waiting for an answer. "Just relax, we are here to have fun, not argue." I don't move from my spot. "I will relax when you tell me what is going on."

"Micah!" A woman screams. She sets the tray down she is carrying and runs into his arms. He picks her up and swings her around. "Sabrina, is that you? When did you make it across the pond?" She laughs in her excitement while I stand there furious. The women he is still holding, wears a skimpy neon pink dress with platform shoes. I can't help but be jealous of her skinny waist.

"Micah, what the fuck?" I glare at them. He drops her suddenly, finally remembering that I am there. "Anna, I'm so sorry. This is Sabrina, my cousin. I haven't seen her in years. Sabrina this is my wife Anna." She looks back in forth between us in shock. "So, it's true, you got married. Aunt Pearl was livid when she got home last night." She states.

"She has nothing to be mad about. I got married, I'm not dead." He slides an arm around my waist and pulls me close. "Men are so clueless. Don't you think your mum would've wanted to see her only son get married? Plus, you never even introduced her. Of course, she is mad." Sabrina has a point; I stick my hand out. "Hi Sabrina, it's nice to meet you. I'm sorry Micah has kept me all to himself. He just can't keep his hands off of me." I smile and she shakes my hand with a knowing look.

"You should come to dinner tomorrow night. Micah has promised to make dinner for his mom. We could get to know each other." Her eyes widen. "Micah is cooking? I think I'll save that trip to the hospital; I have to work anyways. How about another time?" She asks hopefully. "I would love that." She gives Micah a quick hug and then she is gone.

"Okay, out with it." I tell him. "My mum's name is Pearl; she owns this place. That is why everyone knows me. I was surprised to see Sabrina though." I still glare at him. "No, this is not a sex club. Come on, let's have a drink, then we can dance." He pours a glass of wine and a shot of Jack for him. I reach for the Jack and down it before I can change my mind. If I have to be here with him, in his mom's club, I might as well let loose.

He pours another for him and then he leads me to the dance floor. Some people point and some wave hello as we pass. Most of the people ignore us. There is an upbeat song playing and soon we are moving to the beat. I'm not surprised Dr. Image knows all the latest dance moves. With his perfect body and perfect life. He has it all and I'm just plain me, along for the ride.

The next song slows down and he steps up behind me. He pulls my hips close to him. I wiggle my ass, teasing him and I feel every inch of him as he moves with me. My face is getting hot and my body tingles when he kisses my neck. I know I'm playing with fire, but at the moment I don't care.

Suddenly Micah is pulling me from the dance floor. We quickly head up the stairs. "Micah, what's wrong?" He looks over my shoulder. "Katrina is here, let's go." I stop and pull on his hand. "Why don't we give her a show then. Show her you are mine."

A sexy smile spreads across his face. I grab him by his shirt and pull him in. Then wrap my arms around his neck. I kiss him like my life depends on it. He grabs my ass and I feel him hard already. My body is on fire and I can't stop thinking about last night and cuming again. Somehow, we make it up the stairs to our booth. As soon as we are inside, he pulls the other drape closed.

I stand there, not knowing what to do. There is a war raging on in my body. My breathing is rapid, and my panties are wet. Technically we are alone, and no one can see us. We are only supposed to act married, in front of people. I shouldn't want him, but Micah stands there, lust in his eyes, waiting for me to make up my mind. He is the sexiest man I have ever been with. I'm too turned on to listen to my mind. I hesitantly take a step towards him. Then place two hands on his chest and gently push him backwards. He falls backwards on the couch, never breaking his steamy gaze.

Then I slowly climb on top, straddling him. I know I shouldn't, but I can't resist him. So, with my mind made up I kiss his neck as I rub up against him. He pulls down on my hips and moves with me. Micah kisses along the neckline of my dress. This dress is backless, so I'm not wearing a bra. He pinches my nipple and I moan in his ear. "I need you Micah." He kisses me, then pulls away.

"I'm not sure about doing this here." He says and I grind on him. "I don't think I can wait until we get home." I tell him honestly, I might combust. I reach between us and pull on his pants, trying to unbutton them. "Anna, please stop for a minute." I stop and try to calm down.

"I have to be honest with you. While I would love to take you right here, I don't think it is a good idea. I want to make you scream out my name when you cum. But we are in my mum's club. We can leave now, and I can have us home in fifteen minutes. But I'm afraid you will change your mind once we get home." By the time it takes to get there I probably will. "So, what do you want?" He thinks for a moment.

"I want you, more than you know. But I'm selfish and I want all of you, and not just tonight. I want to make you scream my name every night. Make you cum until you can't stand. So, if I fuck you tonight, it will be every night, multiple times. If you say no, we will never fuck again. We can live together and at the end of six months we can go our separate ways. I won't touch you. But if you say yes, I will rock your world." What a cocky bastard. I thought I hated it, but it sounds so sexy coming from his lips.

Chapter Fifteen

I'm not sure about his ultimatum. I'm pretty sure he is serious about never having sex again. I don't like being told no. He is messing with the wrong girl. But, there is no way I can turn him down now. I'm hooked on his sexy as sin body. I climb off of Micah, he looks heartbroken. I laugh a little inside as I pick up the bottle of Pinot. "Can we take this home?" I hold it up. "Sure." He stands up and adjusts his pants. Then he takes my hand as he pulls the drape to the side; still playing his part to the outside world.

We walk outside and wait for the car to be brought around. He looks pissed as we drive home. I can hardly hold it in. I'm just going to make him wait a little longer. We pull up the drive and he parks. He is even a gentleman as he opens my door. I know he is disappointed as I walk upstairs, and he follows. I stop at the top of the stairs.

"Well goodnight Anna. I'll have Nancy make you something to eat." I smirk at his face, always so polite. He turns towards his room. "Micah." He turns around. "Yeah." I smile, holding it in. "I thought you were going to rock my world?" Then I can't hold it in any longer. I laugh so hard, tears stream down my face.

"You little tease." It doesn't take long before he rushes towards me. I shriek and run away. "Little Anna, I told you there is nowhere to run." I duck and slide past him. But he grabs me at the last second and tackles me to the ground. I scream in surprise. My arms are pinned over my head and I can't move. "What am I going to do with you?" I fake innocence. "What's the matter? You said we have to wait until we get home. Did you think I was going to say no?" I tease him.

"You are going to be the death of me. I think someone needs to be punished for teasing her husband." I fake being scared. "No, I'm a good girl." I wiggle against him. "You wouldn't lie to me, would you?" I shake my head no, then kiss him. He pulls away, just out of reach. I can't move to kiss him again. "If you have changed your mind, I can just go to bed alone." I tell him.

Too fast to get away, Micah is off of me and I'm thrown over his shoulder. He picks me up like I weigh nothing. It's only a few feet towards his bedroom and he tosses me on his bed. "Don't move or you'll regret it." He commands and heads to the bathroom. I'm tempted to move, just to see what he does. Instead I remove my shoes and my dress. Then lay there in the middle of the bed; in just my black lace panties and wait.

I don't have to wait long. He pauses when he sees me almost naked. "You're lucky I like what I see, otherwise you would be in more trouble." He stands at the end of the bed and raises his hand. He holds up what looks like the belt from his bathrobe. Asking for permission to tie me up. I nod in agreement; this should be fun.

"You've been a bad girl. Teasing your husband in his mum's club. Give me your hands." I hold them out together. He ties the belt around them tight, but not tight enough that I can't get free. "Lay in the middle." I do as I'm asked. He gently pushes my arms over my head and ties the other end to the bed frame. "Now you really can't run away little Anna." He pulls my panties off so I'm lying there naked, tied to the bed. Then kisses my forehead and walks away.

"Micah! Where are you going?" I yell in confusion. He wouldn't just leave me here, would he? But he leaves his bedroom. "Micah, get back here!" After what seems like forever, he returns in just his boxer briefs. "Little Anna you have been a very naughty girl. Look what I found. I don't think you will be needing this anymore." He holds up a vibrator. Oh my god, is that mine? "Where did you get that?" I ask in confusion.

"Oh, I didn't find it, Nancy did." My eyes widen and then I'm pissed. "What the fuck, she's going through my things now!" I'm so mad, I try to get free. "Relax, I asked her to unpack your things. She just happened to find this." He holds it up and turns it on. "Why would she tell you though?"

He smiles and runs it up my leg. "We don't keep secrets from each other. She found it, so she told me." The vibrator grazes my wet lips. I close my legs, denying him access. "Stop trying to distract me. What else do you not keep from each other? I'm not going to have sex with you, if you're fucking your maid." I glare at him; he turns it off. I try to pull my arms free. He flips me over so fast that I don't even realize it until I feel a smack on my ass.

"Micah, let me go, I'm serious." Another smack, then he rubs that spot. "I'm not going to sleep with you." I say in frustration. He kisses the spot he smacked and continues kissing up my back. I'm trying hard not to let him affect me. But my body is a trader and I moan. His body slides on top of me, I feel his cock at my ass. He kisses my neck and I shiver. "I'm not fucking Nancy, I'm fucking you." He whispers, sliding home. I arch my back in pleasure. Soon, I'm panting as he slams into me over and over. "Micah, don't stop, I'm so close." Two more thrust and then he is gone. The loss is immediate. I turn my head to see what he is doing.

"Micah, come back." He smirks and smacks my ass again. It sends a shock down to my clit. One more and then he turns me over. "I think my little Anna likes that." He spreads my legs and kisses my inner thigh. I hold my breath as I wait for him. He kisses and rubs everywhere but where I need him the most.

"Micah, please." In an instant his mouth is on my clit. I scream out his name as he licks and sucks. My heart is beating so fast, almost as fast as my orgasm is coming. My hips start moving with his mouth, trying to get closer somehow. All at once my body starts to tingle and shake. I'm on the verge of exploding and he stops again.

"What the fuck?" He licks me once more and I shiver. "I didn't tell you that you could cum yet." He states. All of these feelings of desire, anger and frustration overwhelm me. My eyes start to water, and a tear leaks out. "I'm sorry, was that too much?" He wipes it away and unties my hands. He lays on top of me and holds me close and kisses me down my neck. His movements gentle, caressing me. He sucks my nipple, while he plays with the other one. "Micah, I need you." Is my only response.

He slides in, his eyes never leaving mine. It's slow and deep. Way to intimate for quick fuck, with my fake husband. He kisses me and soon I'm on the verge again. "God, I love your body. Don't look away, I want to see you cum." That's all it takes, just his sweet words make me cum so hard I see stars. "Micah." I moan his name. "Anna." He kisses me as he lets loose.

We catch our breaths as we lay there. That was intense, how am I ever going to leave? I want every night to be like this. "About Nancy." I freeze, waiting for the other shoe to drop. "We have not and will never sleep together." I let out a breath, I didn't know I was holding. "How do you know that?" I ask. "Because her girlfriend would be pissed, that's why." Her girlfriend? "Oh my god, she's a lesbian. Why didn't you just say that? Instead of letting me." I stop mid-sentence; I can't admit that. "Because I like seeing you get all jealous." I lightly smack his arm.

"Come on, I'm not done with you yet." He pulls me toward the bathroom and turns on the shower. We can't seem to keep our hands off of each other. We do it in the shower and then on the bathroom counter. I'm exhausted by the time we make it back to bed. I collapse with a satisfied sigh.

Micah gets in behind me and rubs his hand up my leg. "Micah, I'm tired." He kisses my shoulder and down my back. "Do I need to go sleep in my own room?" He pulls away and I lay on my back. He stares down at me. "No, I burned that bed. You are never sleeping in there again. I want you right here next to me every night. He kisses my lips tenderly. "Okay, I'll stay, but I need to sleep." The truth is, I like having his body next to mine. I like it way too much. He nods and I turn on my side. He pulls me close but doesn't try anything else. I settle in and start to drift off. But I could have sworn I heard him lightly whisper in my ear. "Anna, I love you." No, I must be dreaming or delirious from too much sex. I'll worry about it tomorrow.

Chapter Sixteen

The next morning, I wake up and Micah is gone again. I slip on my dress and head to my room to change. I'm surprised that all of the boxes are gone but smile when I see the bed that is still there. I look around the room. My laptop and books are set up at the desk. I walk into the bathroom, the counter has all of my makeup, perfumes and lotions neatly laid out.

The only other door must be the closet. I open it and stare in awe. It's bigger than my bedroom at my apartment. It has custom built shelves and drawers. All of my clothes are hanging up, in color order. It looks like a rainbow of clothes. My shoes line the bottom rack. I slowly walk by looking for something to wear. It's then that I see Micah's dress shirts. I keep going, how long is this closet? All of his clothes and shoes are in here too. The other side of the closet has a door. I open it and end up back in his room.

That's either really creepy or the coolest thing I've ever seen. No wonder why he wanted me to take this room. I turn around and open the drawers on my side of the closet. Then finally find some panties and a bra. Even my jeans are hanging up. I pull a pair down and slip them on, then a shirt. I can't believe Nancy put away all of my stuff, after I was so rude to her.

I grab a book from my desk and head downstairs. The smell of coffee guides me to the kitchen. Nancy has her back towards me as I walk in. "Good morning Mrs. King. How do you like your eggs?" She sets a cup of coffee down in front of me. Then a tray with sugar and cream. I stare in disbelief at her. She is still waiting for an answer. "I don't care, whatever is easier." She turns around to the stove.

"Look Nancy, I think we got off on the wrong foot. I'm sorry for yelling at you. It was wrong of me to accuse you of sleeping with Micah. I'm not normally such a bitch." She places a plate in front of me. "There is nothing to forgive Mrs. King." She goes to the sink and starts washing the dishes. "Please call me Anna, all this Mrs. King thing is driving me crazy. I would like for us to be friends; can you forgive me?" She turns around. "Like I said, there is nothing to forgive. Can I get you anything else?" She asks politely, but I can tell she is still upset.

"No, I don't need anything else." She starts to walk away; I follow her into the living room. "Nancy wait, can we talk for a minute?" She looks down at her watch, impatiently. "I've got like five minutes before the caterers get here with the food for tonight." Oh yeah, his mom is coming tonight. "Do we really need a caterer?" It's just Micah's mom coming right?

"Mrs. Pearl King likes things a certain way. We definitely need them; hell, we need all the help we can get." I plop down on the sofa and start to panic. What am I going to do? I'm just pretending to be married. But what if she doesn't like me? What if she figures it out? I put my head between my legs and take deep breaths. Trying to calm my nerves. "Micah, get your ass in here!" Nancy yells. I hear running and some glass breaking. I still don't move.

"I'll clean that up later, what's wrong?" He must not see me because I'm still bent over. "It's Mrs. King, she is freaking out." Suddenly he is beside me. "Anna, what's wrong? What happened?" He rubs my back, trying to calm me down. "I can't do this." I state. "Do what?" He asks. "I can't lie to your mom. She will see right through me." I take big gulps of air.

"Anna, just relax it's going to be okay." He says softly. "I can't, we should just tell her the truth. Tell her this is all a lie. Then maybe she will understand why I'm helping you. Then she won't hate me." He sits next to me and pulls me onto his lap and holds me. "Shh, it's okay." He whispers.

"How can you say that?" Tears run down my face. "I told you already, I'm a terrible liar." I calm down a little. "So, we are telling her the truth?" I ask hopefully. He doesn't answer right away. "Micah?" He looks strangely at me but wipes away my tears. "Maybe now isn't the right time. I don't want to freak you out even more." My eyes widen, how can this get any worse? "No, I think you should tell me before she gets here. I don't want to look like this in front of her." That would be way worse.

"I told you I've only lied to my mum once. I'm not sure exactly how old I was, maybe seven or eight. I asked my parents if I could have a cookie. My mum said no, but later that day my dad snuck one to me. I didn't want her to find out. So, I made sure to brush my teeth and wipe off my face. When it was bedtime, she asked me if I ate a cookie. I thought there was no way she would know if I lied. My face started turning red and my palms got sweaty. But I still told her no.

She told me she knew I was lying to her. I still tried to deny it. She bent me over her knee and spanked me. Then she grounded me for six months. She took away all of my toys and I couldn't go anywhere. It was a whole year before we even had any cookies in the house. Every night after that, she would set them out on the table tempting me, but I never took one. I didn't want to be grounded ever again. She finally told me how she knew I lied. So, I can't lie to her now either."

"Wow, your mom is tuff. What are we going to tell her then?" I guess we just tell her, we are doing this for his image. "Anna, you haven't been paying attention." Huh? "What do you mean?" He sighs and kisses my forehead. "What do you remember about the night she was here?" They argued, then she left. "You told her I was your publicist and we haven't known each other long. Surely we have to tell her more than that." I state. His grip tightens on me and he kisses me. Our tongues swirl around and I'm getting so turned on just from a kiss. But I pull away from his mouth, out of breath.

"Micah, not now. She will be here tonight. I need to know what to say." I complain, he is not taking this seriously enough. "I just wanted to kiss you one more time before you ran away from me." What? "Why would I run away?" I ask confused. He takes a deep breath. "Because my mum believed me, when I told her I loved you and had to marry you." I freeze in his arms. "Why would she believe you?" I whisper the question, still in shock. "Because I didn't lie." He stares right into my soul. "I love you Anna."

Tears run down my face. How can he love me? It hasn't even been a week. Maybe I wasn't dreaming when he said it last night. I don't know what to say because I don't know what I feel. It's all too soon. People don't fall in love that fast. He doesn't say anything, just waits for me to gather my thoughts. I lay my head on his chest thinking.

He may be cocky as hell and way to good in bed. But do I love him? Is this all about sex to him? I try to remember when his mom came over. No, we didn't have sex yet. It was after they argued. I only kissed him at our wedding. Oh my god, our wedding, it was real for him. It's just now that I finally look at the ring on my finger. It's a white platinum band with a princess cut diamond. On each side of the diamond is an emerald stone. It's quite stunning and something I would have picked myself; if this was a real marriage.

But is it now? Micah told me he loves me. I know I will be devastated when this thing ends. And I hate to admit it, but I'm jealous as hell just thinking about other women he has been with. I want him all to myself, forever. Oh my god, I do love him. I can't believe I didn't see it before. How did this happen? But what do I say now? I'm too chicken shit to admit it aloud. Anna, just pull on your big girl panties and say it.

I raise my head from his chest. He looks worried about what I am going to do. Will I run or will I stay? I'm scared as hell, but he is worth it. "Fuck it, I love you too." He smiles so big; you would think he won the lottery or something. "I can't tell you how happy you just made me. I love you so much." Then his lips crash into mine and I can't get close enough. There are too many clothes in the way. I pull on his t-shirt and he lifts it over his head. My shirt is next. He trails kisses down my neck and pulls my bra cup down. My nipples harden just by his sexy gaze. I moan when he sucks one into his mouth.

"Micah, what about Nancy?" I ask even though I'm nearly incoherent. "Don't worry, she left." He lays me down on the couch and pulls off my jeans and panties. "I can't wait, I need to be inside of you." I couldn't agree more. I stand up and pull down his shorts. His cock springs free. I can't wait any longer, so I climb on top straddling him. I grip him and guide him inside. It's pure ecstasy as I slide down.

Now that I've admitted my feelings, everything feels more intense. Micah's moves are frantic as he pushes up and down. I stare into his blue eyes as I move my hips. He entraps me, I can't look away. "Micah, I'm close." I say breathing hard. He kisses me but pulls away from my mouth just as I start to cum. "Anna, I love you." I feel it all the way to my toes. "Micah, I love you." His eyes roll back in his head when he cums too. He pulls me into a hug, and we sit there for a long time still connected.

Chapter Seventeen

"Is it safe to come in now? The caterers are threatening to leave with the food." Nancy asks from an overhead intercom. I scramble off Micah and he walks over to the wall and pushes a button. "Give us two minutes." We laugh as we rush to get dressed. I'm pulling my shirt down when Nancy walks in. Three men follow her carrying way too much food for just three people.

"Micah, why so much food?" I stare as they come back through, bringing more stuff. "My mum called this morning. Seems she is still mad she couldn't be at our wedding. Wants to have a little get together celebrating us getting married." My eyes open wide. "How many people are coming?" He looks down at his phone checking the number.

"At last count it was sixty-eight." I put my hand to my forehead. I might actually pass out. How did she even invite sixty-eight people that quick? Micah hugs me. "It's going to be okay. We will just tell people it was love at first sight. And we couldn't be happier." I nod even though I'm freaking out inside. The doorbell rings, I here Nancy answer it.

In walks my best friend Sarah. She looks strangely at me for a moment then smirks. "Nice digs, so what's this I hear about a wedding reception?" I pull away from him and turn to hug Sarah. "You have no idea how happy I am to see your face." I tell her and she smiles wide. "Nancy will kill me if I don't clean up this glass. Go talk with your friend. I'll see you in a little while." Then he kisses me on the lips right in front of Sarah. My face turns red as she stares with her mouth open. "I have so much to tell you."

I pull on her hand and lead her into the library and shut the door. "You dirty little whore, you slept with your fake husband." She states, in awe. I can't keep it in, I have to tell someone. "I love him." It comes out in a rush. Sarah's mouth pops open, then she closes it, not knowing what to say. I can almost see the gears grinding as she calculates the time, we have known each other. "I know it's crazy, but we fell in love. Can you believe it?" She shakes her head back in forth.

"Sarah, say something." I demand. "Wow, this room is beautiful." Is all she says. "Yeah, I know it's my favorite." I look down at my shoes. Maybe I am crazy. They better just haul me away now. "Are you sure he loves you back and this isn't some real-life fantasy of yours?" She asks me. I look up. "He told his mom he loved me, before he told me. And that was before we slept together." She is smiling now. "I knew it, you dirty little whore. Well if your happy, I am too." I give her a big hug. "I'm so happy."

"The problem is his mother. She is mad as hell that she wasn't at the wedding and now she has invited sixty-eight people over for a fake wedding reception." I complain. "Anna, you are looking at this the wrong way." I stare confused. "The wedding may have been fake, but it's not anymore. You love each other, right?" What is she getting at? "It means it is not fake anymore.

You really are married; you don't have to get a divorce in six months. You can be happily married and grow old together." Forever? "But what if Micah doesn't want that?"

"Then you clearly don't have any idea how he feels. You should just go ask him, instead of torturing yourself with what ifs." We haven't had the chance to talk about the future. We just admitted our love and hour ago. Maybe he wants me just for now. It will kill me if he wants a divorce. Not after he looked at me and said he loves me when we had sex.

I planned on finding him and asking him right now. But when we exit the library, the house is in full swing of pulling the reception together. Some people are busy hanging lights and decorations. While others clean and move the furniture around. Nancy runs by me, her arms full of plates. "Nancy what the fuck is going on? I thought this was a small party?" She smiles at me finally.

"It was, the list just jumped to one hundred and fifty-two. Mrs. King is insane. I have to run." What the fuck? "Wait, what can I do to help?" I yell after her. "Just go get ready. The guest will be here in two hours." Then she is gone. I look down at my watch, it reads eleven am.

Sarah giggles and I glare at her. "Come on, let's find me something to wear that my mother in-law will approve of." I lead her upstairs to my room and straight into the closet. "I've died and gone to heaven. Just look at the size of this thing." She stares in awe of my closet. "That's what I said about Micah." I tease her. She laughs and then we spend the next hour getting ready. I find a sexy green wrap around dress, that doesn't make me look too fat. Sarah does my hair and makeup. Good thing she came prepared with a dress of her own for the party.

We rush downstairs and I stop in my tracks. The whole house has been transformed with sparkling lights, flowers and silk fabric that billows from the banisters. "Let's see if Nancy needs help." Sarah follows me to the kitchen; no one is in there. The backyard doors are open, so we walk out. I've never been out here, and I didn't realize it was so big. We walk past the pool and see a bunch of tables being set up. White linen covers them and people in tuxedos rush around setting them up and placing centerpieces on them.

I don't know what to do. How did they do all of this so quick? I'm amazed how everything looks. Micah sees us and comes over. "Anna, I missed you. Now don't freak out, I need to tell you something. Do you mind if I borrow her real quick Sarah?" She raises her eyebrows. "Sure, I'm sure someone needs my help." She heads toward the tables.

He leads me down the walk and to the right. The fountain I saw the first day sits in the middle of a flower garden. Only now there are lights around them. He looks nervous as he turns towards me. "Anna, you know I love you." I nod my head. "I love you too." He kisses me lightly. "I know this is quick and it's only been five days. But from the moment I saw you at the hospital. With your dirty mouth, I knew I couldn't let you go." He gets down on one knee. "So, Anna, will you marry me for real? I can't imagine my life without you in it." I stare down in shock. "Shut the fuck up!" He smirks at my outburst. "I mean yes, yes I'll marry you for real. I love you so much." He gets up from kneeling and picks me up. I giggle as he spins me around and presses kisses all over my face.

He stops when he hears clapping behind us. He slowly sets me down and stands straight, almost scared. There is an older woman standing there with a black bob and piercing blue eyes. "Hi mum, I would like to introduce you to Anna. Anna this is my mom Pearl King." I stand there scared as hell. "So, this is the woman who has captured my sons' heart?" She steps forward, I stay still. "Welcome to the family, it's about time I get some grandkids." Then she hugs me tight. I hug her back surprised.

"But I'm not pregnant." She smiles big. "Oh, I know, I just heard that whole proposal. It's too soon to know yet." I grab my stomach and feel ill. I can't be pregnant. She laughs at my discomfort. "Come on, let's get you two hitched for real." I glance at Micah; he shrugs his shoulders. Not knowing what to say about his mom.

That is how I got married twice to the love of my life. Life is wonderful and no I'm not pregnant yet. We want to get to know each other before we bring a little one into the mix. Katrina dropped the malpractice suit when she landed a big movie deal. Turns out she was just jealous of Nancy and thought they were sleeping together. That's an honest mistake, it could happen to anyone.

I convinced my sexy as hell husband to pose for pictures for his website and advertising. In the end we picked the picture he texted me the night we first went out. The one of him in the water. There is a big billboard with his picture that says, Dr. Image. His new slogan. Now he is so busy he has to turn people away. Who cares if he hasn't had any work done on himself. I'm busy myself with new clients. Everyone asks me how I got a guy as sexy as Dr. Image. I just laugh and say he is my King.

The End

Dear Reader,

Thanks for reading Dr. Image. I hope you enjoyed reading it as much as I did writing it. Please help out a new author by leaving a review.

J. M. Willis

About the author……

J.M. Willis is a mother of three sons and has five adorable grandchildren. She lives in Sin City with her husband and she has helped care for cancer patients for the last twenty years. Also, she was Valedictorian of her high school and president of the student council; all while raising a two-year-old. Her husband admits that she is obsessed with Ancestry.com and collecting Disney lithographs, figurines and dolls. She used to hate to read; but now reads a couple of books a week and believes the book is always better than the movie.

Visit my website for more books coming your way. https://j-m-willis-books5.webnode.com
Follow me on Instagram-J.M.Willisbooks
https://www.goodreads.com/jmwillis

Made in the USA
Columbia, SC
04 August 2020